Contents

Just Between Us Girls

An Introduction

What *is* a story for girls? It's a story that only girls can truly feel and understand, that's what!

Interesting as boys are (and aren't they!), they do have a way of being contented with just the surface things in a story . . . the action. Not you, though. You're a girl, and you like to see beneath the surface and find out how the characters feel, why they feel that way, and what they ought to do about it. That's why you'll like *A Batch of the Best*.

These twelve stories are about the people you know best—girls—and their problems with boys and other girls and families. You may even find one of your own problems in these pages—perhaps even a solution to it!

Here are the girls you'll read about:

A BATCH OF THE BEST

CAROL, in a dither over how to be fascinating on the second date of her life, listens to her little sister in a chance encounter with a little boy at dancing school—and learns the very simple secret of success with boys.

ELIZABETH, in a bleak, black mood, certain that she's hideously ugly and unwanted, sets out for a lonely walk. Then suddenly her life takes a whole new direction—all because of something that happens in the park.

NANCY, who wants only to be an architect, gets miserably involved in a project with the sewing class. But good old Nancy comes through, in her own weird and wonderful way!

SUSAN, because of an unfortunate and too-dependent friend, is missing out on all the fun things of high school. How can she do what she must do, without hurting her friend?

FIDELE finds herself competing with her own huge, galumphing puppy for a boy's attention.

MARY needs the wisdom of gentle, dark-eyed Fredo to teach her that she isn't really ready to fall in love with him.

DENISE, feeling rejected in a new school, tries, unsuccessfully, to use baby-sitting as an excuse for avoiding classmates—and one special boy.

FORTUNE meets, under near tragic circumstances, a man she has loved, but hasn't seen, since they were both children.

BETSEY is home alone, during a storm, when the family cat gives birth to kittens. When things begin to go wrong, Betsey uses knowledge she didn't know she had.

CAROLE, unhappily facing yet another wildly unconventional family Christmas, gets a fine, fresh view of her family—through the eyes of a solidly conventional boy.

DIANE—plain, serious-minded, brilliant—learns, when tragedy strikes, that the world needs the pretty, less-than-brilliant girls, too.

ANNE's life is close to disaster because "the family" thinks she and her froth-minded cousin must be, look, and act alike. A sense of humor and a brainy boy come to her rescue.

So—there's a small taste of each story in *A Batch of the Best*. Turn the page and enjoy the *whole* treat!

N.G.G.

Little Sister Will Lead You

Pauline Smith

Beautiful Friday! Carol thought as she dashed into the house. She slammed the back door and leaned against it. *But is it so beautiful?*

This would be the second date of her entire life. The first had been a complete fiasco. With awful clarity, she remembered the strained smile that had glued her lips into idiotic silence—the shyness that had frozen her vocal cords. Carol scrunched her eyes tight against the memory and pushed herself from the door.

"Mom!" she cried as she crossed the kitchen and entered the hall. "Mom, I've got a date!"

"Oh, there you are," came her mother's voice from Franny's bedroom. "Good. In here, Carol."

Mother was distracted. She stood in the middle

of the bedroom, with Franny's ballet slippers dangling from her fingers. "Carol, you'll have to walk her to dancing class."

"Mom, I can't!"

"Of course you can."

"But, Mom, I've got a date tonight!" Carol clenched her fists, thinking of all she had to do in preparation—sit in front of the mirror and practice saying things—write down cute remarks so she could remember them—do that jaw exercise she'd read about so she would be relaxed, for heaven's sake, and sound out with a syllable or two. This was not a sit-around-and-watch-the-submarine-race type of date. This was a real, honest-to-goodness, "We'll-go-to-the-show-and-eat-afterwards-huh?" sort of thing.

And Mother was knocking it. Not that she knew she was knocking it. All she was doing was trying to get Franny to her dancing lesson without taking her herself.

"Mom!" agonized Carol. "My date's at seven. Seven sharp, he said. And I've got a million things to do."

Mother leaned toward the hall and called, "Franny! Now, you hurry." She looked back at Carol and danced the ballet slippers on the ends of their ribbons. "Seven? My dear, it's only three now. You'll be back before four thirty. That'll give

14

"It ain't mine," said the boy. "I like dogs. I got a big one that would chase this cat a mile if he saw it."

"I like dogs, too," said Franny. "But my mom's allergic to them, so I've got a turtle, two fish, and a hamster."

Being unable to compete, the boy blew a bubble.

"Have you ever raised a caterpillar into a butterfly?" asked Franny suddenly.

The boy's mother took her eyes away from the dancers for a moment and rested them on Franny. The boy pondered, working his gum around in his cheek, searching for an impressive answer. "No," he admitted, then added triumphantly, "but I've seen it after it was a butterfly."

Franny shrugged and turned her shoulder.

The boy, anxious to get her attention again, leaned across the cat and poked her. "How old are you?"

"Seven, going on eight," said Franny.

"I'm nine," said the boy.

His mother said, "You are not. You're eight going on nine."

"Who's your best friend?" the boy asked Franny. "Your very best friend. The closest one you've got."

"Me," said Franny.

The boy blew a bubble almost to the bursting point, then gently drew it back into his mouth. "Right," he said. "You see that girl in there?" He pointed toward the viewing window. "The one in red tights and the pink shirt? She's my sister. She likes red and pink together. She likes catsup on bread, too. She eats. You never saw anyone eat so much. I call her the bottomless pit. Do you think you could live on milk, without anything else? I mean milk all alone. . . ."

The dancing class was now lined up and doing acrobatics on the dirty old mat. This was the end of the period. Franny had already slipped off her car coat and was changing from tennis shoes to ballet slippers.

The boy leaned down so she wouldn't miss a minute of his conversation. "I heard of a man once that just lived on milk, and a kid I know down the street's rat had mice. . . ."

Franny straightened. "Rats don't have mice. Rats have baby rats. Do you have a baseball card collection?" She stood up as the dancers exploded from the practice room.

The boy stood, too, talking fast. "I collect bottle caps and stamps."

Franny made for the practice room without a backward glance. "Rocks, too," the boy yelled after her. "And next year I'm going to collect caterpillars so I can raise butterflies. . . ." He was on his toes, shouting over heads.

He turned to his mother. "Gosh!" he said.

"Okay," said his mother. She gave him a little push. She gave the girl in the red tights and pink shirt a little push, too. "Come on, let's go."

Franny and the rest of her class were at the bar, going through their positions while the teacher counted in a singsong voice.

"Come on!" said the boy's mother as she held the door open. The boy clung to the viewing window, dragging his hands along the glass, taking short, reluctant, sideways steps toward his mother. "Gosh," he said loudly. "Gosh, I wish she went to my school. Gosh. . . ." Finally, the door closed behind him.

How did she do it? Carol wondered. She still heard the boy's fervent "gosh." She could still see his reverent fingers slowly sliding along the pane.

How did she do it? No talking into a mirror, no jotting down and memorizing *bon mots*. No anything, except warmth and interest and a beautiful naturalness.

Carol sat up straight, with a sudden revelation. She was watching Franny now as she left the bar and took her place on the practice floor. The music started its bell-like tinkle, and Franny raised her arms, drooped her hands, and bent her head for

19

the beginning of a step. She was no more graceful than any of the rest of those little girls who were just beginning to learn, but Franny was natural, and, without self-consciousness, her awkwardness became enchanting.

That was it. It was her very *naturalness* that had caught the boy's attention and kept it at fever pitch, to be retained even after she was gone.

Carol turned her head so that no one would see and moved her jaws in a tentative exercise; but that was an invention for relaxation, a fabrication for naturalness, and it would not work.

She looked back at Franny hopping around on the practice floor, looking far more like a galloping colt than a ballerina. She leaned over to stroke the cat, a seat away.

A natural warm interest, Carol discovered in that instant, would chase away the shyness that froze her throat and glued her lips together in nervous apprehension.

The class was over. She stood. She helped Franny with her car coat and slung the ballet slippers around her own neck. The coin shop was quiet; a man was hanging a CLOSED sign on the door. They turned and waited for an instant at the driveway of the filling station. Only one car in it—an old Studebaker with painted gold scrolls along the sides, with a boy leaning over the hood

lovingly while the filling station attendant filled
the tank with gas. They started across the driveway.

Carol stopped dead.

That was Glenn Hanson leaning over the hood!
Glenn Hanson, her date for tonight!

Her throat froze. Her face stiffened. She turned
her head and started to walk Franny quickly past
the driveway. Then she remembered. Her nerves
gave one last quiver of protest as she jerked
Franny to a standstill.

"Hey," said Franny.

How had she opened negotiations with the boy
in the dance studio? How? It was the cat, thought
Carol, the cat that lay on the chair between them.

She grabbed Franny and, with the ballet slippers bobbing on her shoulders, walked quickly
toward the gold-scrolled car and the boy who
leaned over the hood.

"Hi, Glenn," said Carol. He looked up; his face
brightened. "That's a real neat car you've got,"
said Carol.

"Sure is." He stroked it. He looked at the car
for a moment, then over the hood at Carol. "I'm
getting it gassed up for our date tonight. Hey,
how about me running you and your kid sister
home now?"

"How about that?" said Carol.

She climbed in and pulled Franny in after her. She relaxed—without any exercises. She patted Franny's shoulder, which surprised Franny, who hadn't the slightest idea that the pat was one of appreciation. Glenn paid the attendant and climbed in on the driver's side without opening the door. He turned on the ignition and roared the motor.

"Gosh!" he said over the noise and started out of the filling station. "Gosh, this is nice, huh?"

"Sure is," said Carol.

They would have a successful date tonight. That Carol knew. No worries, no problems, no frozen-up vocal cords. Just warmth, interest, and a beautiful naturalness. Carol sighed happily. She had it made.

Naturally, she had it made!

Sunday Afternoon

Lucile Vaughan Payne

OUTSIDE THE HOUSE, Vernay Street trembled in midafternoon sunlight. Elizabeth, pausing on her way from the kitchen to the porch, shifted her gaze from the scene framed by the screen and glanced at her watery image in the glass pane of the front door. For a moment she stared at herself stonily. Then her lips curled in an expression of utter distaste. The mouth that was reflected back at her grimaced vaguely in instant response.

Thinking of all the food she had just eaten, Elizabeth shuddered. I'm disgusting, she thought. I have no soul. How can you have a soul and still eat like a horse? Did Heloïse eat like a horse? Did Juliet sit and stuff her face with roast pork and beans and candied yams? Revolted, Elizabeth opened the screen door and walked out. Her mother was sitting in the pillowed swing, her hands folded comfortably in her lap as she watched, with bright, unflagging interest, her own particular stretch of Vernay Street. How can she stand it? Elizabeth wondered. How can she look so comfortable and so *interested*—yes, actually interested! What is there to see? Mrs. Rossiter bending over her flower bed. Simmons's cat washing its face. Nosy old Mrs. Sprunt squeaking away in her chintz-covered rocker and fanning herself.

Sunday afternoon. How I hate Sunday afternoons!

With lowering brows, she watched Rose Marie Rossiter run out of the house and climb into Willie Kline's dusty roadster. She thinks she's so popular.

"Well, young lady," said Mrs. Kane, "what are you up to this afternoon?"

"Up to?" said Elizabeth. "*Up* to?" She spread her hands hopelessly. "What is there to be up to?"

Aware of her too-full stomach, she was smitten with sudden terror as she watched her mother relax placidly on the cushions. I am growing old and fat; soon I, too, will be sitting in the porch swing to watch the march of Sunday afternoons. Her hands curled at her sides. Life is passing me by. Maybe it's just around the corner. Maybe it lurks on Vine Street or Logan or Mackay. It is not here. That much is certain.

"I think I'll go for a walk," she said broodingly.

"My, in this hot sun? Why don't you sit down and enjoy the breeze?"

Because, Mother, this house, this street, this very atmosphere is driving me crazy. Very simply, it's driving me crazy. "No. . . ."

She went down the steps, sauntered slowly down the walk. Beneath her feet the blossoms of the catalpa tree disintegrated, leaving a faint, impalpable odor on the summer air. A fat russet worm made his leisurely way across the sidewalk, and the patterned shade of the trees moved lightly. Dappled with sunlight, the lovely young creature . . . yes, Mrs. Sprunt, I know you are sitting there on your porch watching me. Don't expect me to look up. I will not. I will not!

She looked up and waved vaguely at the old woman. I know what you're thinking. "There goes Elizabeth Kane," you're saying. "Just look at that, getting so grown-up. Getting a figure, isn't she?" Yes, I'm getting a figure, so what about it? "Be sixteen pretty soon, won't she?" *All right!* Say it, say it: Almost-Sweet-Sixteen-and-Never-Been-Kissed. It's none of your business, none of your business, none of your. . . . She passed out of the range of Mrs. Sprunt's vision and felt the tension leaving her muscles. When I think somebody is watching

25

me, my legs begin to jerk, and my neck gets stiff. That's a funny thing. I don't like it. I don't like to have people watching me. It's really none of their business.

Do you suppose I'm the only girl in this town who is almost sixteen years old and hasn't a date? At the next corner, three houses down—that's where Robert Mayo lives. What do you care where he lives? You must not, under any circumstances, Elizabeth, turn your head to look in that direction. He's probably at the ball game or something, anyway. Or maybe he's out with a girl. Jealousy spread through her chest like heat. Some of the girls say he's too shy to ask anybody for a date, but I bet he does; he's just the secret type and doesn't let anybody know.

She raised her head high and crossed the street at Robert's corner, sternly keeping her eyes straight ahead.

What's so wonderful about Robert Mayo? Just another dumb boy. All boys are dumb. Maybe if I walk just as slow as I can, he'll see me, and maybe if he sees me, he'll. . . .

She breathed more easily as distance grew between herself and the corner. She looked furtively at the houses along the street. They were set farther back on their lawns than those in her section, and she saw nobody near enough to hear. She muttered to herself, tentatively, "I love you, Robert." The words had a strange, choppy sound. It embarrassed her to say them. How did you learn to say it naturally? Like those stars in the imported movies. She tried it the foreign way. More "lov" than "love," she decided; sort of between them. "I lov you, Robert." She closed her eyes, floating along the sidewalk. "Oh, dawling, I lov you so much. . . ."

She was swept with sudden laughter and ducked her head, biting her lip to keep the laughter inside herself. They'll think I'm a crazy woman, she thought, darting a glance at the houses lining the street. But saying the words had released something in her. She felt extraordinarily gay and daring, and she began to walk more swiftly.

I shouldn't make fun, she told herself severely. For you know, Elizabeth, down deep in your heart, that it's true. She was touched with gravity. I love you, Robert. As long as she did not say the words aloud, it was all right; they repeated themselves in her mind, deep and thrilling. Oh, Elizabeth, you are in love. How wonderful and terrible it is. She closed her eyes dreamily and thought about it. In love. It was such an enormous thing to think about that it frightened her. But you must face the facts, Elizabeth. Even though it's hopeless, even though others would laugh if they

27

knew, you can be brave enough to admit to yourself that you are in love. It is a far, far braver thing that I do now. . . .

A figure brushed by her, and she jumped, startled. "Oh, hello, Elizabeth," he said.

"Why . . . hello, Robert." My hair! Does it look all right? Is he going to stop? Will he walk with me? If I could only think of something to say, something to make him laugh or something.

He hesitated for only a moment and then rushed on, mumbling about being late. Elizabeth kept smiling stiffly until he had disappeared around a corner, and then her muscles went slack. Her hands were cold and perspiring.

I hate him, she thought passionately. I hate all men. He couldn't stop to talk to me—not even for a minute. She plunged ahead, with set jaw. Finally she realized that she had reached Vernay Park. She had walked with head down, unseeing, and now the green turf stretched on either side of the walk, cool and inviting. Her feet were hot. She stepped into the grass and went toward the trees, still trembling inwardly in a queer way. I'd like to lie down on the grass and pull out handfuls of it, she thought savagely. I'd like to grab the ugly old roots of that elm tree and pull them up and hear them tearing loose from the ground. Perspiration trickled down her scalp and wet the roots

of her hair. She walked aimlessly among the trees, looking for a place to sit down.

"Why, Elizabeth Kane!" a voice said archly behind her. "What are *you* doing here?"

Elizabeth avoided the light, sliding eyes. Sophie Turner—she had forgotten about Sophie Turner. She doesn't have a date, either, thought Elizabeth drearily. That makes two of us. *They are as sisters.* She gagged on the thought. "Going for a walk," she said shortly.

"Well, then," said Sophie brightly, tucking her arm under Elizabeth's, "let's walk together."

If I'm to die, I choose to die alone. "No," said Elizabeth, bending down to tie a shoe that was not untied and freeing her arm. "I can't. I'm meeting somebody."

"I *bet!* A girl or a boy?"

"Well, so long."

"Stuck-up!" Her voice followed Elizabeth. "Anyway, if you want to know, all the fellas are over by the tennis court." Elizabeth felt her face grow red. Can those eyes pierce the sacred fortress of my mind? *Those* eyes?

Bitter with humiliation, she took another direction through the park. Who is this creature all forlorn, unloved, unwanted, and forsworn? I am a marked woman. A poor bony thing who walks through parks on Sunday afternoon, hoping a boy will look at her. Ah, no, I am not like that.

Or am I? Maybe I'm just a coward. Sophie admits it, but I won't. Does that make me any better? Face the facts, Elizabeth. Always face the facts.

It's hot, she thought. She fished a dime from her pocket and went toward the concession, debating whether to buy ice cream or a cold drink. Under the trees a fair maiden passed. She allowed herself a silent snort of cynical laughter. Ah, yes. Ah, yes. Floating like a zephyr on the soft summer air.

At the door of the concession she drew a quick breath and walked quickly away. Robert was inside, drinking a soda. The plate glass windows reflected her image as she rushed by. I'm ugly! she thought in terror. The curl is coming out of my hair, my dress is wrinkled, my nose is too big. They are in there now, saying, "Look at that big, ugly girl." Look at me; my knuckles are too big, and my neck looks scrawny, and the bone in my wrist sticks out like a doorknob.

I never knew before what I really looked like. My arms . . . I saw my arms, long as an ape's. It is only when you see yourself unexpectedly in a plate glass window that you know what you really look like. I saw myself, myself now and myself as I shall be when I am older, an old maid with a jutting profile and big feet and cotton stockings. It was all there.

31

I shall never be happy, I shall never be loved.

She sat down on a stone bench beside the little fishpond, clutching at the rough edge with her hands. If only I were old now. About thirty, thin and tall and dressed in printed lavender cotton that covers my feet. My big, ugly feet. Away, far away from people. I will have a damp, sweet, dark old house at the bottom of a hill, and I shall flit among the shadows, never speaking. If I wear long, full sleeves, nobody will notice my long, ape arms. People will wonder about me but never dare to ask. I shall be remote and gentle and mysterious.

With those big feet?

The sun beat down. Freckles, she thought. While I sit here, the freckles pop out on my great big nose and my hair gets stringy. I'm sweating. I don't perspire. I sweat. Not for me the dainty corner of a handkerchief. Rivers of sweat. "Rivers of sweat," she said aloud, wading in it.

An old woman, her face the color of sandpaper, walked by and glanced at her. She knows, thought Elizabeth. As Sophie knew. When that old woman was a girl, no man ever looked at her, either. We recognized each other. We are kin. Sisters. Horrified, she averted her eyes and flopped down on the grass.

"Well, gee whiz," said Robert, above her. "I was hoping I'd find you here."

She lay quite still and looked at the matted grass. She could see a black ant hauling a bread crumb through the moist corridors among the roots. It's nothing, she told herself. He just wants to know whether I've seen Joe Zilch or something. She tilted her head upward and squinted through the sun.

"Well, hi," she said.

He sat down on the bench and began whittling on a twig. His foot almost touched her elbow. She saw that one shoelace was broken and tied in a knot. A little cascade of shavings began to fall on the grass.

"Do you know what's on at the Lyric?" he asked.

"No." Her heart began to thud, and she swerved her head around to look at the fishpond. A snake doctor was winging around in circles, and she watched it very closely. You think he'll ask you to go to the Lyric with him? Ha.

"It's one of those foreign pictures. You like them?"

"Oh . . . sure." She had to repress a gust of nervous laughter. I love you, Robert.

"Well, why don't we get together? I mean, would you like to see it? I mean, I'd like to take you, if you want to go, I mean. . . ."

Why, he *is* shy! she thought. She felt a casualness, a delightful sense of ease and discovery.

"Why, yes, thank you. I'd love to go, Robert." She got to her feet and pushed back her damp hair. "I was just about ready to go home. Coming?" As easy as that.

"Sure."

And they were walking across the park together. It was no dream. It was real. He asked me, she thought. *He asked me!* She wanted to grab all the trees and shake them and bring the leaves down over her hair. She felt like yelling and singing and running in all directions at once; at the same time, something sweet and sluggish crept through her veins, dragging at her footsteps. They passed the concession again, and the windows reflected their passage. Why, I'm very pretty! thought Elizabeth. I'm almost beautiful. Surreptitiously she gripped one wrist between her fingers and felt the bone and thought how delicate it was, how small.

When they came to Robert's corner, he continued to walk down Vernay Street beside her. With slanted eyes she looked at him, and she began to laugh. Her laughter rang out clearly in the gathering dusk, and Robert looked at her questioningly, the corners of his mouth beginning to twitch.

"What are you laughing about?"

"Nothing. I just happened to think of something."

She liked the way he began to laugh with her,

his eyes curious but friendly. She liked his long, loose-jointed stride as he ranged along beside her. She liked everything about him; she was having a good time, and she was not at all in love.

Willie Kline's roadster came boiling past and stopped in front of Rossiters'. Benevolently, Elizabeth waved at Rose Marie. We'll have to double-date sometime.

"Hello, Mrs. Sprunt," she called gently as they passed the old woman, still sitting on her front porch. How serene and kind she looks, thought Elizabeth. And I wish that I had brought her some ice cream from the concession.

Her own front porch was empty now. Probably her mother had gone inside to get supper on the table. "I'll be back in about an hour," said Robert. "Will you be ready?"

"Mmm-hmm." She watched him go a little way down the street and then went quietly into the house. She was suddenly very hungry, and the clatter of dishes from the kitchen was a reassuring and welcome sound. It was good to be home.

There was no sunlight now to reflect her image from the glass pane in the door. But Elizabeth did not even stop to see. She looked just the same, she knew. Everything was just the same. And entirely different.

Not Exactly
Carnaby Street

Jane Williams Pugel

IT NEVER occurred to me that Miss Volkman—better known at Central as The Volkswagen, because she is so tiny, so tough, and so changeless—had anything earthshaking in mind that Tuesday morning in Home Ec.

"Nancy," she said repeatedly, getting my attention with difficulty. "Would you be good enough to come in after school and discuss the spring fashion show with me? The date has been set, and we have to get busy soon." She smiled what I now realize was a sly smile, although at the time it seemed more like a simple *Mona Lisa* grimace. "And since you always have so much to say about everything, in class and out, whether I am talking or not, I'm sure you'll have some excellent ideas."

"I—" I started to say and accidentally knocked a pile of books off the table. Miss Volkman closed her eyes for a moment.

"After school, Nancy," she said, "after school. We'll talk about it then."

And we did. She appointed me general chairman of the fashion show and added that she thought it would be nice, this year, to sell tickets for the show and raise money for some worthy charity.

"Probably after they see the clothes," I said, "the audience will vote to donate the proceeds for new wardrobes for the models."

"No, Nancy," Miss Volkman said seriously, "there has never yet been a fashion show at Central which didn't do the girls and the Home Ec department proud. I am sure it will be the same this year. And," she added, rather more loudly than I thought was necessary, "I am sure you will be a superb chairman and will turn your many, many talents to this end for the next month."

"Yes, Miss Volkman," I said. I thought a minute. "But, actually, I think Linda or Corry could do a better job. What I mean is, I'm not so good in Home Ec—I haven't even finished ironing the handkerchief I hemmed when I was a freshman, and, well, how can I be chairman of the show when I can't even finish a garment to model?"

"You will have, my dear. You will have," she said grimly and began to shuffle papers on her desk.

"But—"

"Did George Washington say 'but' at Valley Forge?"

"I wasn't there, but—"

"Did the President of the United States say 'but' when he was asked to run for office?"

"My grandfather thinks he should have."

"Nancy, Nancy," cried Miss Volkman, clasping her head for some reason. *"You are chairman of the fashion show. That is all."*

I had a feeling that the dialogue was ended, so I backed away—straight into some chairs which the last class had stacked on the cutting table for our janitor. Miss Volkman kept her hands clasped to her head and her eyes shut until I got out the door. She also seemed to be muttering something. I always seemed to have an odd effect on her.

"I think it'll do you good, honey," Grandma said that evening when I told her about it. "For one thing, you'll *have* to finish a dress, or else you'll be the most embarrassed model in the show."

"Oh, Gran, I'm no seamstress!" I was desperate. "I'm going to be an architect—I keep telling you!

I'll just *buy* the clothes I need."

"Every woman," Grandpa broke in, "be she an architect or a pig farmer, should be able to sew. And that's that!"

I love my grandparents dearly, and I can hardly remember living anywhere else. But sometimes, darling as they are, I think it might help if they were a little younger—or something.

Anyway, I was stuck with the job. Grandma said at breakfast that it would be best to get things rolling right away. So the next day I announced in Home Ec that every member of the class would be required to model a dress she had made.

"And besides modeling," I added, "we'll all have to help out with the other jobs, too. Miss Volkman wants us to raise money with the show this year, and that's going to mean selling tickets *plus* putting on a really groovy show that'll be worth the money."

"Nancy," called Miss Volkman as she picked up the spools of thread I had knocked to the floor as I talked, "I think perhaps you girls should decide today what you would like to raise money for." We finally settled on the Handicapped Center, since we would be raising this money by using our own hands and could contribute something to help others learn to use *their* hands.

We chose a ticket chairman and chairmen for

music, lights, advertising, models, and so on. "Wow!" I said, looking at the list. "If you guys all do your jobs, there won't be a thing for me to do!" Little did I know.

First things first, of course: I seemed to be the only member of the class who had not chosen a pattern and material for my project. I do seem to be able to talk myself out of a lot of things, but I had to face up to this show. I *had* to wear something in the show or be, as Grandma put it, forever embarrassed.

Grandma took me shopping. She moaned and groaned with delight over those huge rolls of material stacked as far as the eye could see in the yard goods department. Apparently I was supposed to fall in love with something and not be able to rest until I had it whipped into a dress. My favorite wearing apparel is the blue jeans and sweat shirt combination.

"Here, now, honey," she said, holding up some blue material. "This looks like you."

"Oh, thanks a lot, Gran," I muttered, staring at the shapeless mass. "You think I should lose some weight?"

"No, I mean the color."

"It *is* nice," I had to admit. Before I could say anything more, Grandma had swept the material and a pattern to the counter, and it was mine.

The cutting out of the dress limped along with the other hair-graying activities I found myself embroiled in. Marge Proctor, who was in charge of tickets, turned up in Home Ec class one morning with tears in her eyes and the neat pack of printed tickets. The tickets, handsomely designed, read:

CENTRAL HIGH ANNUAL
SMYLE SHOW

"Oh, no!" was all the poor old Volkswagen could get out. I thought a minute. I was certain, knowing Marge's printing, that the error was in the copy she had given the printing shop—and we could not afford another set of tickets.

"Well, let's roll with the punches," I said, dropping the pinking shears on my toe and screaming in pain. When I got hold of myself, I said, "Let's advertise it something like—well—SMYLE WITH STYLE." Even Miss Volkman looked approvingly at me, and the ticket crisis was over. But my continuing crisis, That Dress, still remained. I sighed and went back to pinking seams, never one of my favorite pastimes. And my toe hurt.

I enlisted the help of the manual arts department to build our runway. We always hold the fashion show in the auditorium, putting up a temporary runway to lead from the stage through the center aisle to the rear of the room. Mr. Levenson came with me one afternoon and took measurements and all. But I don't think his mind was on his business, for, when the boys began putting up the runway the week before the show, it sloped steeply up toward the back of the auditorium.

"Mr. Levenson," I said politely, when I had finally found him lurking behind a screaming power saw, which made conversation difficult. "Mr. Levenson, the runway goes practically straight up from the stage. Something doesn't seem right."

"But I measured it myself, Nancy; it has to be right." He happily ran another board through his saw, and I inhaled a mouthful of sawdust.

"But it's all wrong," I choked out.

"Well, the trip *out* may be hard on your models," he said, sighting with one eye along his board, "but just think—it'll be downhill all the way home!"

Since you can't really argue with a teacher, I had to let it go. I decided I would simply have to convince Miss Volkman that, with that steep climb facing our models, she would *have* to let them wear their skirts a little shorter than she had decreed, which was just above the ankle, practically.

She finally gave in, after a trip to the auditorium and a view of the Matterhorn the boys were building. The girls gleefully set about turning up their

hems and discussing what kind of panty hose to wear.

Meanwhile, back at the cutting table, I was in real trouble. Grandma had chosen a simple pattern for me, but nothing went together right. The darts darted in the wrong direction; where it was supposed to *ease,* the dress resisted. I sewed the neck facings to the wrong side, so I had a sort of ragged collar dangling out where my neck shot through the hole. It was a sorry thing, but I was the sorriest thing.

Poor Miss Volkman came near to stabbing me with her cutting shears several times, but she contained herself, and we worked hours and hours over that dress, after school and before school, day in and day out.

All the other arrangements were moving forward beautifully, however. I was the only model whose garment was not ready the day before the show. The other girls were delighted over their shorter skirts: not exactly mini, but not as much on the maxi side as they had been, either.

Marianne Boyle, who was in charge of music, had even talked The Moving Teetertotter, our best combo at Central, into doing the music for us gratis. That announcement in the morning bulletin brought a rash of ticket sales. Corry McDonald's mother, who belongs to a lot of clubs, was selling big batches of tickets around town, too. Our big, colorful signs, which the art department had done for us, proclaiming SMYLE AND THE WORLD SMYLES WITH YOU, and SMYLE AWHYLE WITH STYLE, were brightening a good many store windows downtown. The *Citizen* was even running free announcements for us. Things looked good for the Handicapped Center, and for Miss Volkman and the department. Things looked good for everyone but me.

At the last minute, Miss Bethards, the drama coach, who was helping out with lights and giving girls tips on modeling and grooming, also agreed to read the commentary in her velvet tones. It was the final touch of class for the show.

"Grandpa and I can hardly wait for Thursday night," Grandma said on Tuesday. "Honey, you're not eating a thing!"

"Maybe she's on a diet so she'll look like she's been dead a week, the way those model people in the magazines look," Grandpa chuckled.

"Oh, Gran, I'm in a mess!" I burst out. "My dress is terrible, and me chairman of the show. And I'll flunk Home Ec if I don't model, and I'll have this to do all over again next year. I haven't even got the hem up yet, and only one sleeve is in! I don't know what to do."

"Don't give up the ship!" Grandpa called out

45

from behind his paper. "Full steam ahead, girl!"

"Bert!" Grandma glared at the newspaper, then smiled at me. Really smiled. "I know you'll do it and do it right, honey," she said. "You *can* finish the dress. You'll be the prettiest model there. *You have it in you not to quit.*"

Her words cheered me a little. Maybe I *could* do it—do it for Gran and justify her faith in me. I went into my room and snatched that miserable heap of material off the bed and set to work. I worked feverishly all the next day, crying with frustration much of the time. Architecture had never looked so good to me.

I put the last stitch in the hem, the last snap at the neck, ten minutes before show time. I could hear The Moving Teetertotter going full blast, the buzz of voices in the audience. The first models were going on. I wildly pulled on the chartreuse panty hose I'd fished from a drawer without looking. I had been so busy finishing my dress and coordinating ticket sales, music, models, and The Volkswagen—who was wheeling around backstage even now in high gear—that I hadn't had time to think about accessories for myself.

"Why, Nancy, *green* with that brilliant blue dress?" Miss Volkman squeaked, clasping her hands over her eyes as I straightened up and rammed my head into an open cupboard door.

When I regained my composure, I said coolly, "Sure, Miss Volkman. They're—well, in—it's what everybody's wearing on Carnaby Street." It was the first thing that came into my head; I was a little desperate trying to salvage that passing mark in Home Ec.

"Well, this is not exactly Carnaby Street, but— if you say so, Nancy." She smiled. I could almost hear her thinking that if her luck held ten more minutes, she *might* be rid of me next year. She began to put my dress over my head, and then— "Good grief!" she shrieked. "This sleeve is in upside down!"

That almost did it, for both of us. I wished I could faint, but I've never been able to.

Finally I muttered, between clenched teeth, "I'm going to model this thing, anyway—you've got to pass me and get me out of here." So I finished putting on the dress and kept my right arm straight up, since that's the way the sleeve pointed.

"I have it!" cried Miss Volkman, and she thrust an umbrella into my upraised hand, pushed a huge yellow rain hat onto my head, and grimly worked my feet into tall, black patent boots. She found a shiny orange shoulder bag somewhere and hung it on me, then gave me a mighty shove onto the stage just as Miss Bethards's smooth voice began, "And next we have Nancy Markham in—" and I knew she had glanced up.

I staggered up that steep climb, grinning insanely and holding my umbrella high, and she got hold of herself. Her voice held a laugh.

"Here comes Nancy now, very Carnaby Street —Nancy, who is general chairman of this wonderful benefit—modeling her own A-line blue wool. She's ready for a rainy day stroll. . . ."

The Teetertotter began a shaky ad-lib version of "Singing in the Rain," and I went up that mad runway and down again, umbrella high, shoulder bag swinging.

And then I heard the most marvelous sound: smiles turning into happy laughter, then waves of applause. Above all the other noise, I heard Grandpa shouting, "Full steam ahead, girl! Sock it to 'em!" And I caught a glimpse of Grandma's beaming face—just happy, not surprised, for she had known all along I could do it.

Somewhere in the back of my mind, I realized that I had passed Home Ec and pulled off the fashion show and was on my way toward a nice quiet career in architecture.

The Friends

Sofi O'Bryan

SUSAN MANNING deliberately delayed putting away her notes after the buzzer sounded, even though her feet were itching to run out of the classroom and to her locker for her math book and next class. But Tricia was standing in the doorway, her pale face accentuated by her light hair, waiting.

Go away, Susan wanted to shout to her. *Stop waiting for me after every class.*

Mr. Meyers looked up at her questioningly now. Susan knew she had to leave. She picked up her books and walked toward Tricia.

"What took you so long?" Tricia smiled, unaware of the seething rebellion inside her friend. Susan glanced sideways at Tricia, a sharp retort

49

on her lips, but the sight of Tricia's clumsy brace stopped her words. *I can't,* she thought in agonizing frustration. *I can't treat her just like any other girl. I can't—she's crippled!*

Instantly she was sorry for even thinking the word. "Here, let me carry your book," she said to Tricia, taking the thick blue notebook and adding it to her own pile. She walked slowly beside Tricia, close to the wall to escape the oncoming tide of students, and she felt as though no one else in the world had ever faced such a dilemma.

She had known Tricia last year because they had shared two classes, English and gym, but Tricia had never been her friend in the sense that they phoned one another or met after school or visited in each other's home. She was just a classmate. They spoke, and they met in the hallways and lunchroom and in classes, and that was all.

Shortly after spring vacation, Tricia had begun to complain after every gym class that her legs ached. In the rush to dress in the locker room, no one paid her much attention. Once Susan did say, "Tell Miss Smith; she'll excuse you from gym if your legs ache." She wasn't really concerned with Tricia's problem; she was anxious to hurry to the next class and maybe get to talk to Peter Simms.

A few days later, Tricia had fallen while running after a ball in gym, and the teacher told her to have a checkup about the leg pains.

When she didn't come to school for a few days, Susan didn't exactly miss her; she was only vaguely aware that she was absent from class. Then she heard that Tricia was in the hospital with a mild case of polio.

"Polio! I thought no one got polio anymore!" Susan had remarked to someone. She felt faintly sorry for Tricia and chipped in for flowers to send to her in the hospital, but her life had never revolved around Tricia, and soon the girl was completely out of her mind.

There had been other things to occupy her that spring. Peter Simms began to go steady with a girl named Phyllis Newton, and Susan avoided going to the lunchroom with Phyllis, because she knew Peter would be waiting for her near the doorway. And a boy named Sherman started calling her at home, asking her to go to a Saturday afternoon movie. "Why," she wailed to her best friend, Dora, "does the wrong boy always like me?"

Susan had been glad when school ended in June, because then Phyllis wouldn't be seeing Peter anymore, since he was going away with his family. But the summer as a whole had been boring as she and Dora plowed between their houses or to the pool or to Lucafell's candy store.

Tricia wasn't mentioned once, nor was there

any need to think about her.

In August, Susan trailed around the stores after her mother, buying sweaters and underclothes and shoes for school.

"You'd think," she complained to her mother one day, "that I was going to the moon, or they were closing all the stores in September!"

"You'll be glad we shopped early, while the best selections were to be had," her mother said calmly.

Susan returned to school in high spirits. Vacations, she and Dora had decided, were fine for little kids, but maybe it'd be better not to have such a long summer hiatus, when you had nothing really exciting to do. At any rate, Susan saw Tricia on her first day back at school. Momentarily, she was taken aback when Tricia came up to her in homeroom, smiling eagerly.

"Hi," she said. "What's your schedule this term?"

Susan couldn't help noticing the heavy brace on Tricia's right leg and how she had to swing her body around when she moved. She wanted to say something.

"You look great," she said. "I'm glad you're back."

"Oh, this." Tricia thumped her leg on the floor. "I made up my mind nothing was going to stop me from being here today. The doctor said I can get rid of this after a while and use a cane. It's not so bad."

Susan honestly felt she had never met a more heroic person, and she imagined that deep in Tricia's eyes there were hidden pain and a new kind of understanding. She went out of her way, that first day, to try to be helpful to Tricia.

Now she wondered whether that had been her first mistake. To be kind, to be charitable—those were virtues taught her in school and by her parents. But for how long? And at what cost to her own life?

Walking along beside Tricia in the hallway now, she felt as though she were trapped. Just yesterday, she'd started to hope she and Peter might discover each other. It had been after math class, when she leaned over to copy his homework notes and he chatted away with her. Then they both got up and started for the door. Susan's heart jumped wildly—he might even walk her to her next class!

But there was Tricia in the doorway, waiting. "We'll be late," she said, joining Susan as they walked into the hallway.

Peter hesitated a second, then said offhandedly, "Well, see you, Susan." And he loped off after another boy, calling out, "Hey, Rocco, wait up."

Susan watched him go as she paced herself to

53

Tricia's slow gait. If it had been Dora beside her, she could have just walked away with Peter; Dora would have understood and faded into the background. Susan thought, *I could do that to Dora, walk away from her and not feel guilty. But I can't do that to Tricia because of her affliction.*

Tricia was chattering away beside her. "Will you slow down, Sue? I can't keep up with you," she said.

Susan slowed down, biting her tongue. How often lately had she wanted to turn to Tricia and say, "I have to hurry" or "I'll see you later"—as she could do to her other friends? But always she forced herself to remember that Tricia was not like the other girls.

That night at dinner, Susan was pensive—so much so that her mother chided her about it.

"What is it this time—biology?" she asked.

Susan looked at her mother. Perhaps a mother had the answer. She spoke hesitantly about her problem.

"It's not that I don't like her; she's very likable and all that, but she clings to me so!"

"Honey," her father said, "you can't very well refuse friendship to a girl who needs it. Besides, I can't really see that it harms you in any way to slow down for a less fortunate human being. I

54

think what you're doing is fine. I'm proud of you!"

She stared at her father and then down at her mashed potatoes. What else had she expected him to say? On the face of it, her problem was insoluble. No one, unless she were a heartless beast, would hurt someone afflicted as Tricia was.

She saw herself spending her entire tenth-grade year trailing after Tricia from class to class, while the entire school rushed past her and Peter stopped knowing she was alive.

The following Monday, Susan had a biology quiz for which she had studied hard on the weekend. She noticed that Tricia wasn't in homeroom, but Tricia was often late and was generally excused, because it was difficult for her to walk to school, and she often had to wait for a ride. In biology, Susan concentrated on her quiz and felt particularly happy about the results. As she prepared to leave class, she realized, with a sudden surge of freedom, that Tricia hadn't come to school. She started for the door when Peter joined her. Together they began to walk down the hallway.

"How'd you do?" he asked her.

"Okay, I hope," she said. "I sure studied hard enough."

"I did, too, but I blanked out on the second part. Hey, where's your sidekick today?"

Susan felt her heart twist.

"What do you mean?"

"Tricia," Peter said. "She's always trailing after you. No kidding, she kind of gives me the creeps. . . ." Then, quickly, he added, "Don't get me wrong; not because she's crippled or anything like that. She just latches on, if you know what I mean. I had some time ducking her last year. . . ."

Susan turned to look at him. She felt she had to defend Tricia. "She's pretty brave, coming back to school with that brace and all," she said.

"Oh, sure, I know that." He grinned, and his face lit up, and his blue eyes were clear and bright. "It's just that . . . well, I didn't know you two were such buddies. Every time I look around, you're together."

But we're not, Susan wanted to cry out. *We're not really buddies or even best friends. It just happens that she clings to me, walks with me after each class, waits for me at my locker after school.*

"Well, hey, here's my class." Peter paused. "You got biology club after school?"

"Not today," Susan said.

"I'll meet you out front then," he said casually. Susan continued to her own class in a warm glow.

Usually Tricia was with her when they came out of school, and there was always Tricia's mother, waiting to drive the girls home.

"No trouble at all to swing around Jane Street, dear," she told Susan more than once. Susan was too polite to refuse, especially when she didn't have a good reason. The only way she escaped it was to stay after school, but she couldn't do *that* every day, either.

But this afternoon, she was alone, and Peter was waiting for her out front. As she walked toward him, Dora called out to her. "Want to come over to my house for a while?"

Susan shook her head. "No, thanks, I'm going to walk home with Peter."

Dora grinned and walked away toward another girl. As she joined Peter, Susan thought, *I'll call and tell her all about it later.*

And then it suddenly struck her with the force of a blow. She had not included Dora in this walk, nor had she felt she should. But if it had been Tricia, could she have turned her back on her so easily? No, of course not. Tricia would have come limping toward her, and she would have felt duty-bound to include her.

Not because I like her or dislike her or she's special or important in my life, Susan thought, *but because she's handicapped.* That simple truth shocked her into analyzing further: *But that's not fair to Tricia, either! I'm not really giving her a wholehearted friendship, and I might even be keeping her from finding someone who could give her that.*

Peter was talking to her, and she turned a dazzling smile on him. Suddenly she felt lighthearted and relieved. She knew exactly what she must do.

"Hey, what'd I say?" Peter laughed, taking her arm and tucking it under his. "The magic word or something?"

Susan nodded. "I'll tell you about it someday. Isn't it a beautiful day?"

"Want some ice cream?" he asked. "It's only forty degrees."

"I love ice cream in cold weather," she said as they turned toward the candy store.

The next day, Tricia was back in school. She walked with Susan to their first class, and Susan slowed her gait to match Tricia's. Tricia chattered on about her cold and schoolwork, but now Susan didn't mind. She listened to her, not because she was a cripple but in spite of it, and she knew that what she was going to do would be best for both of them.

The minute biology class was over and the students stormed the door, Susan stormed with them. Even when Tricia called out, "Wait, wait!" she didn't wait.

"I have to run," she called, feeling cruel and heartless as she plunged into the hallway.

She felt someone grab her arm. "Hey, what's the rush? You can get expelled for running down a hallway."

It was Peter. She saw Tricia out of the corner of her eye, limping out of the classroom and coming toward her.

"I want to stop off at my locker," she said to Peter. "I have to rush."

"I'll rush with you," he said, taking her arm.

Susan was painfully aware of Tricia's being left behind. She forced herself not to look back. She got to her next class just as the buzzer was ringing. Tricia was already in her seat, right next to Susan's. All through class, Susan was heartsick about what she had done and didn't look at Tricia once. When the buzzer sounded this time, Tricia leaned over and said to Susan in a hurt voice, "Thanks for waiting for me!"

Susan looked at Tricia. It was now or never. Tricia just couldn't be allowed to go on using the fact that she was a cripple. She would always remain a cripple then, not just in her body but in her mind, too.

"I can't walk with you after every class, Tricia," Susan said slowly and deliberately. "I've forced myself to wait for you because of your leg, but it's not fair to either of us. Pretty soon neither one of us will have any other friends." The hurt was plain on Tricia's face, but Susan forced herself to continue. "There's nothing wrong with you, just because your leg is in a brace. But you're going to make all the kids avoid you if you play it up. I thought you were plenty brave to come back to school this fall, and I still think so. But I can't cater to you . . . I don't want to anymore."

She thought Tricia would cry. Susan's own face turned pale, and she picked up her books hesitantly. For one wild moment, she despised herself and wanted to pick up Tricia's books, tell her to forget what she had said, and walk along with her to the next class. But she saw Peter hovering in the doorway.

"Peter's waiting for me," she said to Tricia, just as she had said it to Dora. And she felt good about putting Tricia on the same level with Dora. That was the way it should be.

She walked toward Peter. "Hi," he said, glancing back toward Tricia. "You alone?"

Susan nodded. He fell into step beside her. Susan did not look back, because she had the wildest notion that, like Lot's wife, she would turn into a pillar of salt or something.

She was in her next class ahead of Tricia. She avoided watching Tricia limp into the room and go to her seat. Math had never been her best subject, and this day was a total loss for Susan. She wanted only to escape this awful feeling that she had kicked a puppy.

When the buzzer sounded, she gathered up her books. Covertly she watched Tricia, waited until she had gone out of the room, then followed. Halfway down the hallway, a girl was rushing past Tricia. Then she stopped, turned, and grinned. She slowed down and matched her gait to Tricia's.

Susan felt her heart lighten. Maybe it was a straw in the wind, but there had to be a beginning somewhere. Perhaps she had been too harsh on Tricia, but she had been just as harsh on herself, she decided. The coward's way out would have been to go on and on, eventually disliking Tricia and herself and harming both of them.

That night at the dinner table, her mother remarked about her good spirits. "Something good happen to you today?"

"Something very good," she said and then excused herself to jump up and answer the telephone.

It might be Peter or Dora or Laurie—or someday Tricia, calling like any other friend to chatter away about boys. That kind of friendship would be a real one.

The Sensational Type

Shirley Shapiro Pugh

FACE IT," said Grandma at breakfast. "I've been here for three weeks, and Fidele hasn't had a date."

"Oh, Gram—" Fidele objected. "Don't—"

"Well, you *are* seventeen years old, and you *are* a good-looking girl," Grandma said flatly, "and you know what the trouble is?"

"I—"

"You are too ladylike," said Grandma.

"Mother, for heaven's sake! What a thing to say to the child!" Fidele's mother gasped.

"Lydia," said Grandma, "you may sit there looking horrified, but you'll admit that's a pretty fair description of what is wrong with Fidele."

"I wasn't aware that anything is wrong with

63

Fidele. Just what *is* wrong with her?"

"Now, let's not get huffy, Lydia. When a girl has hair the color of butterscotch and good brown eyes and nice legs and is seventeen years old, she ought to be creating a sensation *somewhere* along the line."

"I'm just not the sensational type. How can you create a sensation when you just aren't the sensational type?" Fidele asked in her well-modulated, sweet voice.

"Well, you could do a lot of things," said Grandma. "But there isn't anything so terrible wrong with you, honey. You just aren't *young* enough." Grandma, at sixty-four, wore a gray tweed skirt, and a deep red cardigan over a white blouse. Her white hair curled haphazardly around her tanned face. When she did wear a hat, it was never a very dignified hat; she was more likely to wear yellow string gloves than white kid ones. For all her sixty-four years, she managed to create an impression of youth more vividly than her ladylike granddaughter! Not that Fidele was mousy or somber or anything at *all* that you could put your finger on. It was simply that her hair stayed neat in a breeze, her loafers never turned over at the heels, she didn't giggle—her poise was beyond her years and certainly beyond the years of the boys who knew her. She had been a precise little girl, and, although it is doubtful that anyone with hair the color of butterscotch could reach the precise spinster stage—well, she *was* missing a lot of fun right now.

"I think I'll send an escort up here for you when I get home, Fidele," Grandma announced that afternoon. "A sort of decoy."

"You mean a boy?"

"Yes. Yes, might as well be a boy. One of them ought to be ready to travel by now," mused Grandma. "You think you could use a twelve-week-old puppy?"

"You mean a love-me-love-my-dog policy will take years off my personality?"

"With the puppy I have in mind, I can practically see your personality in rompers."

"Let's not go too far, Grandma; but I could use a pup. At least I could take long walks at night, protected."

"Honey, you lay in a supply of dog food. You have a real good chance of becoming the sensational type overnight when this pup arrives."

"What is it, for heaven's sake?"

"Fidele, you put your trust in an old lady. We'll let the breed be a surprise, and if you aren't dated up for the weekend thirty days from now, you can trade him in on a nice cat."

Grandma had belonged to her local Kennel

Club for at least fifteen years; she had had a French poodle, a Peke, and a wirehair that Fidele could remember—and always two Irish setters. All of her dogs were obedience-trained, by herself, and she had a sizable collection of ribbons and trophies won in both obedience trials and dog shows. There were no canines whose temperaments Grandma couldn't describe to would-be dog owners, and Fidele felt sure that whatever breed her "escort" was going to be, Grandma wouldn't go wrong in choosing him.

"Ship him up," Fidele agreed. "Mother will have a fit, of course. When my cocker died, she said that was the end."

"I'll take care of her. You just have to promise me you'll take this puppy for a daily walk, a good long one, and he's yours—collar included."

Grandma left. Fidele bought a leash and waited. Four days later, the express office called Miss Fidele Manning.

"Lady, you got a teddy bear down here," was what the man said. "You want to pick it up, or you want we should bring it out on the truck?"

"I'll come down," she said. "I'd rather carry him home myself."

"Lady, you ain't gonna carry this dog home," the voice informed her. "This here dog weighs a good thirty pounds."

Thirty pounds? Grandma must have sent an older dog, Fidele decided. Well, then, it would be easy to slip a leash on him and walk to the car. Probably Grandma had sold herself on a house-broken, leash-broken dog, and it was going to be much easier to warm Mother up to that idea.

"Mother, when you order the groceries get a couple of cans of dog food," Fidele said, by way of heralding the dog's arrival. "Three cans ought to do for today and tomorrow. Monday we can get some more—he might not like one kind."

"Didn't Grandma tell you what to feed him?"

"No, but I think he'll have some instructions in his crate."

Fidele slipped into a white shirt and a black corduroy jumper and went out to the car. She drove to the express office, her curiosity at the boiling point. Springer spaniel? Nothing sensational about that! Not a boxer. No, not a boxer. Teddy bear, the man said. She ran through a mental list of fluffy breeds: Collie? Some sort of wolfhound? No, Grandma wasn't that theatrical. She parked a block from the express office—as close as she could get. Quickly she walked to the office.

"You have a dog here for Fidele Manning?"

"Hey," said the young man at the window, appreciatively, looking at her with a long, careful look. "Are you the one that dog belongs to?"

"Yes, I am. What do I owe for freight?"

"You don't owe nothing. Prepaid." He called, "Johnson, bring that big dog out here!" In a moment the crate was set before Fidele. Her precocious poise slipped. She fumbled with her thoughts.

"Oh, my golly—I—it's a—"

"That's *some* Saint Bernard dog, lady," said Johnson. "How old is it?"

"Twelve weeks. He's almost up to my knees, isn't he?"

"Sure is." Johnson looked at Fidele and grinned. "Lucky dog!"

Grandma, you were so right! thought Fidele. She said aloud, "I'll walk him to my car and skip the crate. It's not a permanent one." She clipped her leash to the pup's collar. His coat was a giant-size lamb's-wool powder puff, with patches of orange-gold on white. His white-tipped tail flicked tentatively.

"Good pup!" Fidele scratched him behind one ear. "Come on, little dog." She tugged gently on the leash. Too gently—no give! "Here, boy," she insisted, with a slightly less gentle pull. The pup moved his barrel-shaped body a foot forward. His very sad eyes accused her. Fidele stooped and sat on her heels to reassure him that the leash wasn't going to be so bad. With an impetuous bound, he threw her off balance and licked her face as she sat on the floor.

"Hello!" someone's surprised voice greeted her. Fidele looked up to see Ted Walley staring at her in disbelief. Ted would have sworn Fidele Manning would not be anywhere, at any time, sitting on the floor. "If it isn't Fidele Manning, sitting on the floor," he remarked brightly. "Your dog?"

"Present from Grandma." She pushed the pup from her lap with both hands and rose awkwardly. "He's not leash-broken, and I guess I'll have to carry him to the car." She put both arms under the pup's body and lifted him. She felt the unmistakable snap of a slip strap parting from its slip. The pup squirmed and wriggled his forelegs free, which left him dangling from Fidele's arms by his hind legs. She lowered him to the floor. "He's sort of big," she exclaimed.

"He's wonderful," Ted declared, between laughs. "Let me take him to your car, as soon as I pick up a duplicate statement here for Dad."

"I'd appreciate the help." She brushed ineffectually at the fine white fuzz that covered her black jumper.

Ted, Fidele, and the pup covered the block to Fidele's car in less than twenty minutes. Very slightly less, but less. Part of the twenty minutes was spent on Ted's maneuvering the enormous puppy into a carryable position. Several of the twenty minutes were spent talking to people: a little boy who wanted to touch the teddy bear; an old man who had had a Saint Bernard as a child; a middle-aged lady who thought the dog was the cutest thing, and was he part chow? The rest of the twenty minutes was spent coaxing the pup to walk on his leash, because, as Ted conceded, "You can't carry an amorphous mass as big as a full-grown footstool!"

When finally the girl and the dog were settled in the car, Ted suggested, "If you're not busy tonight, I'd like to come over and wrestle with your mutt."

"I'll be busy," Fidele assured him, glancing ruefully toward said mutt, who had begun teething on the seat cover. "But stop by anyway." To herself she said, *Grandma, it's later than you think!*

Fidele smirked rather pleasantly at her mother, who was hurriedly mixing a quart of cooked oatmeal with the remaining half can of dog food. The pup had gulped two and a half cans of food in five minutes and was sniffing expectantly around the kitchen.

"We can't have our baby hungry," Mother said.

"*Our* baby can't possibly be hungry anymore. Look at his sides; they're fat as a blimp's."

"He's the sweetest thing I ever saw. That pretty face!"

"Mother, I think you're taken in!"

"Aren't you?"

"Yes, and I'm not the only one. He's quite a dog," Fidele said. "Snagged me a caller already."

"He what?" Her mother's eyebrows wrinkled into a frown.

"He and I have a boy coming to call this evening, due to an unladylike performance of mine."

"Don't take Grandma too literally, Fidele."

"Well, it wasn't on purpose, but I did take her literally this morning, and it turns out she may not be kidding."

"You're talking in circles. And your slip shows."

"I am? It does?" Fidele, with un-Fidelelike flippancy, whirled across the kitchen floor. The pup scrambled clumsily after her, slid on the waxed linoleum, and skidded into the wall, nose first.

Ted Walley helped name the pup. He and Fidele explored the possibilities of "big" and all its synonyms; probed each other's memories for proper nouns having to do with the Alps (no results); considered any number of screamingly funny ideas that weren't funny the second time they tried them out loud. Late in the evening, a postman arrived with a special delivery letter from

71

Grandma. The postman eyed Fidele's nameless pup suspiciously.

"Will he bite?"

"That's it!" Ted said decisively. "Willie Bite."

"No. No, of course he won't bite," Fidele assured the postman.

Grandma's letter included instructions for feeding: to start with, a pound of horsemeat and a pound of dry dog meal—every day! The scrawled P.S., which Fidele did not read to Ted, was, "Thirty-day trial! You, too, can be irresistible!"

Willie Bite was the dog's name, and when you call a Saint Bernard by name, he perks his ears and inclines his head to one side and looks at you quizzically. Fidele was stopped on the street by three or four people each day on her terms-of-the-gift dog walk. Two out of three of them prefaced their remarks about the pup with "Will he bite?" And each time, Willie Bite returned their steady gazes, cocked his alert ears, and tilted his head, as though to ask, "What for?" He shook hands spontaneously and indiscriminately and any old time. He licked small children's faces from ear to ear, often to the horror of their mothers. He had the usual accidents in the house, and Fidele had to remind her mother that he was not as grown-up as his size, so excuse it, please. Willie Bite led

Fidele into a series of indignities and embarrass-
ments, as any puppy will lead his mistress—but his
size attracted attention to every escapade as no
other pup's could. And whoever looked at the dog
looked at the girl on the other end of the leash!
Fidele was the object of laughter and of awe; she
found herself walking faster than she wanted to,
stopping suddenly when Willie Bite came to a
quick halt for something sniffable. Most of her
clothes were a little less neat than they had been
in her pre-pup days. Fine white fluff accumulated
on them faster than she could brush it off. A big
pink tongue left wet spots at her hemlines, where
her outsize puppy nuzzled against her legs and
drooled.

Ted Walley loved that dog. Of course, in order
to see the dog, he had to see the girl—and, actually, she was quite a girl. Ted was not alone in this
discovery. Everyone knows a boy's best friend is
his dog—or somebody else's dog. Willie Bite intro-
duced any number of boys to Fidele, boys who
had known her all along but had never really
looked at the butterscotch hair or the brown eyes.
Oh, success came slowly, as it usually does, but it
was success. It wasn't going to be necessary to
trade the puppy for a cat in thirty days—not at all.
But Willie Bite's success was *too* successful.

Ted and Fidele played with Willie Bite at home.

73

They taught him simple obedience and trimmed his whiskers. Ted and Fidele took him walking—or was it the other way around? Ted and *Willie Bite* were the pair, and Fidele was on a leash—was it that way? That's the way it was.

You can't go to a school dance on a leash—not if you're a dog and not if you're a girl. And Fidele had come to the point where the dance wasn't going to be interesting in the least unless Ted Walley took her. The competition was terrific—it was Willie Bite. Ted couldn't see the girl for the dog. He looked into brown eyes and said, "Nice expression!" But the brown eyes were Willie Bite's.

Doesn't he ever notice my *nice expression?* thought Fidele.

"The color of butterscotch!" murmured Ted.

That's me! Fidele hoped. But it wasn't. It was Willie Bite, losing his puppy fluff and growing his grown-up coat; his thirty pounds had become fifty-five, and he was four and a half months old, and Grandma was coming to see him.

"Let's give him a bath," Ted suggested. "We can do it with the hose outdoors. The weather's warm. When's your grandmother coming?"

"Sunday noon," Fidele told him.

"Let's make the bath Sunday morning."

"Oh, goody! Let's!" Fidele's voice had an unfamiliar, brittle tone.

"What's the matter with *you*?" Ted asked.

"Nothing. Is something the matter with me?"

"Is Sunday morning okay?"

It was fine. A warm Indian summer morning; and what could be finer for a boy and a girl and a dog? No—a boy and a dog and a girl.

Fidele wore blue denim shorts and a white shirt, nothing on her feet, and something on her mind. Ted wore jeans and a T-shirt and a great big smile of anticipation for a morning with his favorite date —his big, furry, favorite date.

"Willie Bite'll be dry by ten o'clock," Ted remarked as he dragged the hose into the side yard, behind the tall hedge. "What time do you meet the train?"

"Twelve five," Fidele answered. "Here, boy!" She urged the pup toward her. "Turn the water on slow, Ted." She picked up the end of the hose and drizzled a thin stream over Willie Bite. "Come on, boy. You gonna get pretty for Grandma?" Ted turned the water to a full, steady spray and began to rub soap over Willie Bite's neck.

"Look at that big old face," Ted said lovingly.

"Look at that long tail," Ted said.

"Look at that clumsy old paw," Ted said. "We'll have to enter him in the puppy match October twenty-first."

"That's the date of the dance!"

"Look at that floppy old ear! Who's taking you?"

"The Lama of Tibet. Why?"

"No reason. Look at that wet old boy!"

"I said the Lama of Tibet!" Fidele shouted.

"You did?" Ted turned his head just in time to catch the full force of water from the hose squarely in his face.

"Excuse me!" yelled Fidele. She turned the hose down on his head. "Why don't you take me, you—you—*dog lover?*" She aimed the water at his shirt. "Look at me!" Ted wiped his eyes to look. She sprayed the water in his face again.

"What the devil are you doing?" Ted hollered.

"I'm getting you all wet. No, I'm not. You were all wet before I started!"

"Why, you—" Ted grabbed the hose and took aim. Willie Bite ran a circle around them, barking and trailing suds.

The car door opened and Grandma stepped out. "Thank you again," she said to the Conrads, picking up her overnight case. "They'll be so surprised I drove in early." She walked toward the house. "Hello!" she called. "I'm early!" Then she peered around the hedge. A young man seemed to be kissing Fidele. They were both quite wet; in fact, dripping wet. Fidele's Saint Bernard was

77

chasing his tail, in a crazy effort to lick some soap-suds off of it.

"I thought I was early," Grandma muttered. "Hello," she called again. "Looks like I'm right on time!"

The Blue Promise

Loretta Strehlow

No ONE KNOWS exactly where they came from or what they were doing in Banning so early in the year. Usually the migratory workers didn't arrive until harvesttime. Then they came in caravans that pulled up to the dormitory buildings beside the cannery to disgorge brown-skinned children, straw-hatted men, dark-eyed women, and white-haired old people. The Sandozas, in an ancient but highly polished Packard, arrived quietly and all alone, in the first green-gold week of June.

The car lumbered up the hill and groaned to a stop in front of our house. Slipping from behind the wheel, a thin, dark-eyed man approached my father and bowed deeply in a curiously graceful gesture.

79

"I am Alfredo Sandoza," he said, smiling. "We have come to find work." His smile disclosed two gold teeth that gleamed proudly in the Midwestern sun. "We thought you might know where help is needed."

While my father ticked off the names of the surrounding farmers, my sister Kate and I surveyed the Sandoza family. We had seen Mexicans before, but always working in the fields or arm in arm in the stores on Friday nights—never so still, solemn, and quiet.

There was a handsome woman, plump and erect, in the front seat. Two boys' heads, identical in every detail, reared up close to her; and in the backseat, beside a myriad of boxes and household goods, were two girls, one about twelve, the other close to my sister Kate's eight years, and a slender boy, perhaps a year or so older than my sixteen years. His skin was a rich olive, his black hair long and curly. The boy and woman had a secret look about them. The whole family seemed poised to burst into smoke and fire to escape the quietness that bound them to the car and the stillness that was Banning.

I didn't see any of them for nearly a week after that, although Mr. Aldrich, who owned the farm next to ours, had let them move into the small frame building on the edge of his field. Mr. Sandoza and the boy were to help until Mr. Aldrich's hired man recovered the use of his broken leg.

I was in the backyard when Kate came spinning around the corner in pursuit of a windmill of a child—all arms and long legs.

"We saw Conchita that day in the car, remember, Mary?" Kate said as they ran over to me.

The little girl smiled up at me—the same smile, with the exception of the gold teeth, that her father had used so effectively the week before. Conchita stayed all afternoon, wearing the older girl's, Teresa's, shortened skirt and a faded, cut down shirt that must have once belonged to the boy Fredo. It was because of these raggle-taggle clothes that I became involved with the Sandozas.

"It would be a good way to get the closets cleaned," Mother agreed to my suggestion, "if the Sandozas won't be offended."

By the time Chita left for home, we had three boxes of our used clothing and one of toys piled into Kate's old wagon. I felt good that afternoon, almost like a missionary, when I thought of how pleased the Mexican family would be. Chita ran ahead of us, so that by the time Kate and I stopped in front of the house, Teresa and Mrs. Sandoza met us there.

"Look, Teresa," Chita called, "for you." Pulling an old green blouse of mine from the pile, she tossed it in her sister's direction.

Shy at first, Teresa quickly struggled into the blouse, pulling it on over the one she was wearing and whirling around to catch her reflection in the window, just as the Packard ground to a stop beneath a tall oak.

"Mr. Sandoza!" Kate walked out to meet him. "Mary and I . . . we brought some things for your family."

Mr. Sandoza let her take his hand and lead him to the wagon. Mrs. Sandoza had fished one of my father's shirts from the pile. She smiled, a slow smile that started at one corner and took a long time to cross her broad face, as she held the shirt to her husband's thin shoulders.

"It's too big, *Mamacita*." Conchita grabbed the shirt and danced with it to the car. "For you, Fredo," she screamed, tossing the shirt through the open window.

As if by instinct, the boy reached out to catch the shirt. His fingers touched the material almost with a caress, until he saw us watching, and then, slowly, deliberately, he loosened his grip, letting the shirt trail in the bare dirt.

"Alfredo!" Mr. Sandoza's voice was sharp. He turned to us, but I couldn't take my eyes from the boy. He was flushed and angry, the high bones of his cheeks standing out sharply in the lean face.

"I thank you for my family," Mr. Sandoza said. "They will enjoy. Fredo"—his voice held command —"will drive you home. It is late."

Mr. Sandoza lifted the empty wagon into the trunk and handed the keys to Fredo. Fat braids flapping, Kate crawled into the front seat. I slid in beside her, and we swirled onto the road.

Kate chattered away, but Fredo and I were uncomfortably silent, and, strangely pleased as I was to be near him, I was happily relieved when we reached home. My father was there, and Kate ran up the steps toward him, while I turned back to Fredo. Perhaps he was not really so handsome, but, with his smooth gold skin and ragged dark hair, he was completely unlike any of the Banning boys I knew.

"Thank you." I forced my face into a stiff smile. "It wasn't really necessary. . . ."

He didn't look at me. "And it wasn't necessary," he said slowly, "for you to come to us." He turned to me then, dark eyes no longer angry but holding a strange sadness he didn't expect me to understand. "Because we are Mexican does not mean that we need charity."

As soon as Kate's wagon had been lifted from the trunk, he spun the car away from me, heading home. I walked over to my father. He looked at me for a long time, and I knew he had heard Fredo, but he said nothing, only brushed a hand against my cheek as we walked to the house together.

Once a month, in the summer, Banning still has an old-fashioned pavement dance. One whole block of Main Street is cordoned off, and an ancient wooden bandstand is pulled to the middle.

"The Sandozas are coming tonight," Kate said on the way to town. "Chita says she can dance. Do you think she can, Mary? Maybe," she teased, not waiting for my answer, "maybe Fredo will ask *you* to dance."

My mother swung around sharply toward my sister. "Don't be silly, Kate," she said. Then, as she turned back, I could see the glance she exchanged with my father.

"We'll meet here in an hour," Mother said, indicating Mr. Carter's popcorn wagon before she left to shop. Kate scooted for the bandstand. The hour passed quickly, leaving me flushed with the victory of escaping heavy-footed Billy Southworth. I didn't see any of the Sandozas until I was pushing my way toward the popcorn stand. The touch on my arm was so light that, at first, I didn't acknowledge it; but Chita tugged again, and I turned to face her and Fredo.

Fredo, his black hair brushed and dampened in a vain attempt at controlling the thick curls, stood

84

stiffly near the high curb. He had never said he
was sorry, never apologized for what he had said,
but buttoned tightly around his throat and pushed
carefully into his neatly pressed blue jeans was
one of my father's white shirts.

Chita smiled up at me. "Where's Kate?" She
whirled around, giving her brother an unexpected
push that sent him stumbling toward me.

Just then the loud voice of Billy Southworth
cut through the crowd. I was so excited and uncer-
tain over Fredo that I was almost happy to see
Billy, until he threw a tight arm around my waist
and pulled me toward the dancers.

"I'm sorry, Billy." Wriggling loose, I turned
back to where Fredo and Chita stood. "I have to
wait here."

"All right, Mary." Billy stepped back onto the
curb, while some of the boys formed a ragged
semicircle around us. "Have some popcorn, then?"
I was about to agree, when Fredo, moving forward to break the circle, reached for my hand.

"Maria has agreed to have popcorn with us," he
said.

Billy, completely taken aback for the moment,
watched us move toward the wagon. After Fredo
had dug into the pockets of his jeans for the three
dimes, I took the bag he offered and chewed vig-
orously, hoping the crunch of the hot corn would

drown out the comments of the circle of boys.

"Where'd *he* come from?"

"Rest of the Mexes won't be here till harvest."

I wanted to explain that Chita and Fredo were my neighbors and my friends, that my father had helped their father find work, but I couldn't find words.

"Where's your guitar, Mex?"

Chita, her popcorn still untasted, stood pressed against her brother's legs, her black eyes riveted uneasily on Billy.

"Hey, I bet the band don't know we got a Mex here." Billy nudged one of the boys. "But it looks like Mary does. Right, Mary?"

I still don't know why I moved weakly away from the Sandozas, when all I really wanted was to support them and to turn my back on Billy and his friends, but I did leave them, and I did not answer Billy.

"I am Mexican, as you say," Fredo said lazily, as though Billy had asked the question of him. "And you are right . . . everyone knows that Mexes play the guitar." The small knot of people around the wagon were openly staring, and even some dancers drifted over to listen. "And everyone," Fredo continued loudly, his eyes flat and dark with the same proud anger I had seen before, "everyone knows we go barefoot, sleep on the floor, and eat beans with our fingers."

Conchita was crying then, a silent sobbing that shook her thin shoulders. Fredo stared at me for a minute, as though he were waiting for me to say something, but when I didn't speak, he turned away. He lifted his sister around the waist, and the two of them stepped into the circle of dancers.

"She *can*," Kate's little-girl voice whispered beside me. "Chita can dance."

We watched them dip and swirl, the tall dark boy and the little girl, both as stiff and unsmiling as mannequins.

My parents said nothing on the way home, but I was sure they knew. I was glad not to talk, but, long after the house was dark and silent, I thought about what had happened and the things I might have said and done. I finally fell asleep to the perfume of red clover and the drifting strains of a guitar being strummed somewhere in the dark.

Our first meetings after the dance were awkward, but we lived so close, and Kate and Conchita became such fast friends, that somehow it seemed impossible for Fredo and me not to be friends, too. Though I was always strangely embarrassed whenever we met on the streets of Banning, ease with Fredo seemed to come naturally away from town.

When June ended and July came in, with its heat and its burning blue skies, we fell into the habit of meeting at the creek just after supper each night. Kate and Chita would wade to the middle of the shallow stream to pick up smooth, white stones for the twins, while Fredo and Teresa taught me to braid the long meadow grass into baskets. I learned that Fredo and Teresa had been born in Mexico, but Chita and the twins in Texas.

"In those days we had some land," Fredo said, "but the drought came, the wheat burned, and the cattle died."

"And we've been moving ever since. But I remember"—Teresa smiled wistfully—"that once I found a turquoise on our land."

From his pocket Fredo took a blue green piece of stone. He turned it in his hand, and I could see that, though it had never been polished, it was worn smooth with handling.

"I keep this one," he said, "for good luck. Maybe it will lead us to land again."

Thinking back, I'm sure that I was the last to realize how important Fredo was becoming to me. Even he knew it before I did. He must have, otherwise he wouldn't have been so prepared for that last evening, for the things he had to say to me.

School was only a week away, and we hadn't

been to the creek for three days. When Kate and I cut through the meadows, I was afraid that Fredo might not be there, but we heard his guitar and the sound of stones skipping.

"Kate!" Conchita ran up the bank to throw her arms around us. "Kate! Maria! We're going home!"

Kate scrambled down the bank, while I turned to Fredo. His brown eyes were solemn; his dark hair was neatly combed, as though for a special occasion.

"The Aldriches' hired man is back. There is no need for all of us to stay."

"But where will you go?"

"South again. West. Maybe—" he took the blue turquoise and held it to the last of the light—"maybe we will be able to buy land again."

The twins, fat legs dangling in the water, smiled up at me. Teresa and Chita, shouting and giggling, chased Kate up the opposite bank, where the three of them rolled hilariously in the long grass. It seemed impossible, somehow, that they should be so happy, because suddenly, with a shock that almost stopped my heart, I realized how bleak and how empty my life would be without Fredo.

"Do you *have* to go?" The words stuck in my throat, and I couldn't even look at him to see if he had heard.

"Yes," Fredo said slowly. "Yes, I think so."

"But my father would give you work," I cried.
"You could stay."

"No, Maria. No."

My chest felt tight with the weight of his words,
until, at last, I could stand it no more. I flung myself at him, brushing the strings of the guitar, so
that my admission was accompanied by a disso-
nant chord.

"But I love you, Fredo. I love you!"

Mildly astonished at the tears in my voice, the
twins looked up from their tower of pebbles. From
the opposite field, the girls' voices, sounding thin
and lonely, drifted back to us. Fredo slipped an
arm around my shoulders, and I buried my head
in the softness of my father's old shirt. He didn't
laugh or tease me. His voice was soft and full.

"I am proud of that," he said.

"Please stay." Once started, I seemed to have
no control over my words. They spilled and tum-
bled like water down his white shirtfront. Finally
I leaned back to look at him.

"My father," he said dreamily, rubbing the
smooth turquoise, "had land once, Maria. But
owning land and working land for someone else
were very different things, and so he lost it. One
day, when he is ready, we will have land again,
and it will be better than the first time because
now my father has learned."

I didn't understand what this had to do with us, but the girls were crossing the stream again, and one of the twins clambered up the bank to hand Fredo a choice pebble. The first stars were rising above the meadow, and it was time to go home.

The Sandozas left two days after that. I didn't say good-bye or watch them go. Instead, I slipped across the meadow to the creek, where even the water was silent and waiting, waiting, as I was, for the music and the laughter that the Sandozas had brought to its banks during the short, short summer. It was there, placed carefully to crown the little mound of white stones, that I found the turquoise, gleaming like a blue promise of love to come.

My father told me later that Fredo could have stayed if he had wished. Mr. Aldrich had offered him a permanent job. But I'm glad now that he chose not to stay. I think he must have known that, when school started again, I couldn't be the same, that I was still weak enough to be forced back into the world of Billy Southworth, still afraid to pit my feelings against blind prejudice. I would be like his father—a landowner before I was ready.

Later, love will come again—that's what the turquoise was meant to say—but in a different time and a different place, when Mary Cullen becomes a woman. When I am that woman and do fall in love (as I'm sure now I will), some memories will fade and blur; but the reasons for remembering that wonderful summer are so poignant that, even without Fredo's sea blue token, they could never be forgotten.

Mr. Dillon
Rides Again

Lorena K. Sample

DENISE MITCHELL scooped her English notes into her notebook and hurried toward the door before anyone could notice that she was not included in any of the small, chattering groups. She turned reluctantly when she heard Mrs. MacMillan call her name.

"I was hoping you would stay for our Creative Writing Club meeting this afternoon," Mrs. Mac-Millan said. "Your themes show a good deal of writing ability."

Denise glanced at Joanne Kent and the little group surrounding her, and she wished desperately that one of them might at least second the invitation.

"Thanks, but I have to get home and take care

of Mr. Dillon—that's Matt, my little brother—this afternoon," Denise said. "He—he needs me. My mother isn't home much."

"Perhaps some other time, then."

"Perhaps." *But it isn't likely*, Denise added to herself. After six weeks at Westwood High, she still felt like an unwelcome stranger, and she was not about to barge in on any of the snobbish little clubs. She had never been any VIP back at South High, but there, at least, she'd had friends and dates; she'd belonged.

At her locker, she ran a comb through her hair, slipped into her jacket, and slammed the door. A tinkle of shattered glass followed the slam.

Cole Langston, pulling a letterman's sweater out of his locker two doors away, grinned at her. "You'll be old enough to vote before you run out of bad luck."

Ruefully Denise reopened the locker and surveyed the glassy splinters from the mirror which had been taped to the door.

"You hold a sheet of notebook paper under the door, and I'll brush the pieces out," Cole said.

After the mess was deposited in a trash can, Cole walked down the hall with her. He was of medium height, with a husky build, and had an indefinable air of being better dressed than the boys at South High.

"Thanks for helping me," Denise said. She slowed as they approached the main bulletin board near the front entrance, wishing she could think of something witty and interesting to say, but her mind was as empty as a scrubbed blackboard.

"How do you like Westwood High by now?" Cole asked.

Denise stared absentmindedly at the bulletin board as she tried to think of some just-right reply. Westwood High girls always seemed so self-assured, always knew exactly the right things to say and do and wear. Suddenly Denise realized that she was staring directly at a big poster announcing a letterman-sponsored dance and that Cole's gaze had followed hers. He probably thought she was openly angling for an invitation!

"I have to hurry," Denise said abruptly. "I have to take care of my little brother this afternoon." She fled, and the tide of embarrassment had barely begun to ebb by the time she called for Mr. Dillon at the nursery.

He was easy to spot among the children playing in the airy, comfortable room. At three and a half, he was already taller and huskier than many children approaching kindergarten age. It was his size and his habit of greeting people with feet widespread and gun hand poised, added to the fact that his name was Matt, that had early earned him the nickname of "Mr. Dillon."

"Pow," said Mr. Dillon.

"Pow," returned Denise. "Ready to go home?"

"Okay."

Mrs. Wheeler brought his sweater and cap, and then they walked the four blocks home together. It was an area of lovely homes with nicely kept yards, and Denise's new home was as nice as any of them. She thoroughly loved her turquoise and white room, but she couldn't help wishing the whole house and lot could be picked up bodily and plunked down on Holly Street, where they had lived before.

"Shall we go over to the playground today?"

Mr. Dillon stuffed an interesting-looking winged maple seed into his pocket and scowled. "Freddie don't want to go playground."

Denise sighed and realized that it had finally come to the point where she must discuss "Freddie" with her mother.

"Let's coax him," Denise suggested. She addressed the imaginary Freddie. "How about it, Freddie? You and Mr. Dillon can swing and slide and have lots of fun."

"Okay," Mr. Dillon said finally, without much enthusiasm.

"Tell me about Freddie," Denise suggested.

97

They passed the house and continued toward the playground in the park. "How old is he? What does he look like?"

Mr. Dillon ended the conversation by simply ignoring the questions until they reached the park.

"What would you like to play on first?" Denise asked. "The slide? The Thing?"

"Freddie don't want to play on Thing."

"Must we always do just what Freddie wants to do?" Denise asked, more puzzled than annoyed. "You used to love to play on the Thing."

The Thing was made of red and yellow plastic. It had holes to crawl through, dips to slide down, short tunnels to hide in. It was by far the most popular piece of equipment on the playground.

"Come on," Denise coaxed. "Let's go play on the Thing."

The look of absolute panic on Mr. Dillon's face startled Denise. He ran to an empty swing and started pumping furiously. Denise pushed him, and he seemed to enjoy himself after he calmed down, but she couldn't erase from her mind his strange display of fear.

Mrs. Mitchell was home by the time Denise and Mr. Dillon got there. She had slipped a smock on over her office clothes, but she still looked poised and efficient. Denise momentarily considered talking with her mother about the unfriendliness at Westwood High, but she doubted that Mrs. Mitchell would understand. Mrs. Mitchell, as a teen-ager, had been elected everything from cheerleader to Spring Queen to Drama Club president.

"You had a call a few minutes ago," Mrs. Mitchell said. She picked up Mr. Dillon and hugged him, and he squirmed delightedly.

"Who was it?"

"He didn't say. Do you have a date tonight?"

Denise's heart leaped momentarily. Could the caller have been Cole?

"Aren't you and Dad going somewhere?" Denise asked, skirting the question her mother asked. "I thought I'd take care of Mr. Dillon. And I do have a lot of homework."

"Well, perhaps we will run over to the Morrisons' if you're going to be home anyway," Mrs. Mitchell said. She opened a can of mushrooms and sprinkled them into the sauce on the stove. "I never can think of any excuse to get out of these things when you're around to care for Mr. Dillon."

"Oh, I might as well take care of him," Denise said lightly. "I haven't nearly as much to do here as I had at South High. It's kind of late in the year to get started in activities and things."

"Oh, I see."

"About Mr. Dillon," Denise began, changing the subject as she selected silver for the table. "Have you ever heard him mention a Freddie?"

"Ummm, I don't think so. Why?"

Denise explained about the imaginary Freddie.

Mrs. Mitchell laughed. "Oh, I don't think it's anything to worry about. Lots of children invent an imaginary playmate. We're just lucky he didn't invent a Doc or a Festus or a Kitty to go with his Mr. Dillon name."

"But *why* would he invent someone?"

"I suppose we should investigate that," Mrs. Mitchell agreed thoughtfully. She tasted and then seasoned the green salad. "I think it probably indicates that Mr. Dillon is an unusually bright boy, however. It takes an amount of intelligence to invent an imaginary playmate."

Denise agreed that Mr. Dillon often did seem very intelligent for his age, but his size made him look considerably older than he was, and Denise knew that people sometimes thought him not so bright.

She was just snapping his sleepers together when the phone rang, shortly after her parents had left. It was Cole Langston.

"I know it's late to be calling," he said, "but I thought maybe you'd like to see a movie—" It wasn't exactly phrased as a question, but there was an upward lift at the end. "I tried to call earlier."

"I'm sorry, but I'm taking care of my little brother tonight," Denise said. "My parents went out."

There was a short pause before Cole said, "You must take care of him a lot."

With sudden intuition, Denise realized that Cole wasn't quite sure he believed her. He thought she might be making up the story because she didn't want to go out with him!

"My mother has an interior decorating business, so I pick up little brother at the nursery every day and take care of him until Mom gets home," Denise explained. "And then I take care of him evenings, when Mom and Dad go out."

She didn't add that it was the success of her mother's interior decorating business that had made the move to the expensive Westwood section possible or that when they lived in the South High area she seldom took care of her brother, because she usually had a date.

"It's really not work," she went on. "I take him to the playground almost every afternoon, and we have lots of fun. He even has an imaginary playmate named Freddie."

"Oh." Pause. "Well, I'll be seeing you, then." Click.

Denise swallowed hard and managed to turn

101

her hurt into anger. That was a snooty Westwood boy for you—calling for a date at the last minute and never bothering to ask if you might be available some other evening.

The weekend dragged, as weekends always did lately. There was a game Saturday night, but Denise didn't go. *Why should I care if Westwood wins or not?* she asked herself.

Sunday was rainy and blowy, but the sun was out by the time Denise and Mr. Dillon walked to the park Monday afternoon. The playground was almost deserted, and raindrops still sparkled on the unused slide.

"The Thing looks almost dry. Why don't you play on it?" Denise suggested.

Freddie, who had disappeared for the weekend, suddenly sprang to life. "Freddie wants swing."

"Let's play with Freddie on the Thing," Denise said. "Come on—you take one of Freddie's hands and I'll take the other, and we'll just walk right over to that old Thing."

Mr. Dillon watched, fascinated, as a little boy about his own age swooped out of one of the Thing's exits. It really did look like fun, Denise thought suddenly. Her glance darted around the empty benches.

"How about if I play on the Thing, too? Would Freddie come then?"

Mr. Dillon nodded, but he hung back until Denise crawled through one of the entrances. Then, together, they swooped down the dips and crawled through the tunnels. Denise had a moment of crazy panic, when she thought she was caught in one of them. Suppose the fire department had to come and rescue her and it was in all the papers— How could she ever explain *that* at Westwood High? She was still giggling to herself about it when she slid out of one of the Thing's exits—and there, looking right at her, was Cole!

"Well, hi," Denise managed to say. Her hair was all mussed, and her plaid skirt was turned sideways, and she felt like an absolute idiot.

He grinned. "Can one more play? Or maybe this is a private game."

"Aren't all games *and* everything else in Westwood private?" Denise snapped. She pushed futilely at her hair.

"You're not exactly a model of friendliness yourself," Cole returned. He shoved his hands into his pockets. "You act as if you can hardly wait to get away from school every day."

"I explained that I take care of my brother." She spoke with greater dignity than she felt as she tried to straighten her skirt and succeeded only in twisting it around, so that now it was completely backward.

103

"Yeah. Well, I guess you did." Cole looked half-way apologetic, and Denise wondered if he had passed through the park at this particular time to see if she really did come to the playground with her brother. "Is your brother in there with his imaginary little friend?"

"Freddie—that's his imaginary friend—comes and goes. He just appears when my brother doesn't want to do something." With a little shock of surprise, Denise realized that was exactly the way it was. It was only when Mr. Dillon was dragging his feet about doing something, usually about playing on the Thing, that Freddie's opinion was voiced.

"What do you do—borrow Freddie part time?" Cole asked, but Denise hadn't time just then to wonder what he meant.

A howl of terror echoed from the other side of the Thing, and two boys, perhaps nine or ten years old, darted out of it and dodged past Denise and Cole.

"That was Mr. Dillon!"

Cole looked at her as if she must have had too many spins through the Thing, but she didn't take time to explain about her little brother's nickname. She raced around the yellow and red modernistic form and found Mr. Dillon screaming on the far side. Denise put her arms around him.

"It's all right, hon. Are you hurt? What in the world is wrong?"

"Did he hurt himself?" Cole asked.

As Mr. Dillon's sobs finally quieted, Denise inspected him for injuries, but she could find none.

"Please, tell Sis what's wrong," she begged.

"Thing *eat* me!" Mr. Dillon sobbed finally.

"Eat him! Is that what he said?" Cole asked.

Denise nodded. "Well, the Thing surely isn't going to eat you, hon. It's just an old pile of plastic—see? Let's touch it. Whatever made you think it eats people?"

"Boys said." Mr. Dillon's mouth still turned down.

"Freddie?"

Mr. Dillon shook his head violently. "Real boys."

"Maybe the boys who ran by us just before he started crying," Cole said. "I'll try to find them."

"But he's been afraid of the Thing for days," Denise said. She wiped Mr. Dillon's face with a handkerchief while he edged away from the Thing. She also explained briefly to Cole about Mr. Dillon's nickname.

"Hey, there go those boys!"

Before Denise could stop him, Cole jumped up to run after the boys. He caught one by the arm, and, after a sharp exchange of words, both boys accompanied Cole back to Mr. Dillon and Denise.

"Tell Denise and her brother what you told me," Cole ordered the boys.

"We're sorry we scared you," one boy said finally, addressing Mr. Dillon. He wore jeans and a striped T-shirt and had a rolled-up comic book in one hip pocket. He glanced at Denise. "We just wanted him to get out of the way so we could play." He turned back to Mr. Dillon. "It don't really eat anybody like we told you. It's just a bunch of dumb old plastic."

"It's just a story they made up," Denise tried to explain to Mr. Dillon. "Do you understand, hon? Not real. It was just something they made up, the way you made up Freddie."

"Did you kids ever tell him this crazy story about the Thing before?" Cole asked suddenly.

The boy kicked at an island of grass in the sea of worn dirt. "Once. He's just a scaredy-cat, or he wouldn't of believed us, anyway."

"He's big for his age," Denise said gently. "He's only three and a half."

Both boys looked startled and apologized again, and finally Cole let them go. He sighed. "Now I suppose they'll rush home and tell their mothers all about the traumatic experience *they* had, and someone will come and jump on me."

"Well, come home with us, and I'll give you a

107

Coke to fortify you for the ordeal." It was what Denise would have said to one of the boys at South High, but now her eyes widened. You just *didn't* invite one of the most popular boys at Westwood High home for a Coke, when you had never even had a date with him. "I mean, *sometime* . . . that is, if you want to . . . I mean, I guess Mr. Dillon and I had better be running along now, so thanks for your help."

"I take it you're withdrawing your invitation. Was it just a slip?"

"Well, it's an error no one at Westwood High would make, isn't it?" Denise snapped. "No one there ever slips and invites an outsider to anything."

"Such as what?"

"The Creative Writing Club. The—"

"Who even knows you're interested in creative writing, unless you make an effort to act interested? Who knows *anything* about you, in fact, when you're about as friendly as that statue of Grant at the other end of the park? Come on out from behind Mr. Dillon and act like a human being."

At the mention of Mr. Dillon, Denise suddenly realized he was gone, but a moment later his face reappeared in the Thing.

"Pow," he said.

"Well, Mr. Dillon rides again," Cole commented. "How about you?"

Perhaps no one had told her Westwood High ate strangers, but Denise knew she had been acting as if she thought it would. She had been deceiving herself more than anyone else when she said Mr. Dillon needed so much of her time; it had been she who needed *him*, because she was afraid to get out and try to make new friends of her own. Mr. Dillon was really just as happy staying at the nursery until Mrs. Mitchell got home. And if Cole Langston thought she had acted unfriendly, most likely a good many other people at Westwood High thought so, too.

Denise took a deep breath and finally blurted it out. "The offer of a Coke is still open."

Cole grinned. "Accepted," he said. "And I have an offer of my own to make, too—unless, of course, you have to take care of Mr. Dillon and his imaginary friend the night of the lettermen's dance."

"I think the imaginary friend may be gone for good," Denise said. "And I think Mom may be glad to have Mr. Dillon to herself for a change. I've rather monopolized him."

It was going to be scary, Denise thought, actually *trying* to make friends at Westwood High. *Scary, but nice,* she added, eyeing Cole Langston's cheerful profile.

The Gift
by the Wagon

Dorothy M. Johnson

AFTER A WHILE Caleb understood that he was
sick, that he had been sick quite a long time. The
simmering pain in his shoulder had been a boiling
pain, he remembered dimly. So he must be getting
better. And someone had been looking after him,
but he did not know who it was or why they should
be doing it or how he was going to pay for it.

There was a medicine smell, but that was on
himself. Beyond it was the smell of horses, and he
was bedded down on hay. He worried for a while
and then wavered dizzily back to sleep.

Later he heard a girl's voice. "I could look after
him if you'd move him to the house."

And a man's. "It wouldn't be fitting. Anyhow,
he's too sick to be moved yet."

"Did he say anything about who he is or who shot him?"

"I don't know any more than you do. A ragged stranger without a dollar in his pocket."

Ragged, yes. But rich, too. The shock of realization made Caleb start and hurt his shoulder. Then the gentle warmth of knowledge crept over him: *I've got fifteen thousand dollars banked with Wells Fargo. That's why I was dry-gulched back there somewhere. The men figured I was taking the gold out myself.*

When the man came again and put a hand on Caleb's forehead to test the fever, Caleb asked, "Where is this place?"

"Livery stable in Fenton," the man answered. "Fort Fenton, it used to be. My boys found you in the pasture. Thought you were dead."

Caleb murmured, "I came a long way, then, after I was shot."

A long way I rode—must be ninety miles—with the fever blazing. And what brought me this direction in the first place? I wanted to go back ten years and prove to somebody that I amounted to something, after all. Somebody who probably isn't here anymore, and I hated her, anyway, because I was a coward and she wasn't.

He wanted to call out to the man, "You needn't give me charity. I can pay you well."

111

But he knew that was not true. You cannot balance a debt of kindness with a poke of gold any more than you can subtract three pigs from five apples. He was in debt to this man whose name he did not know, and the thought angered him.

The man did not know him, either; the man looked after him; that was all. *Charity,* Caleb thought. *It's a burden to me.*

He found out the man's name: Pete Wilson; he ran the livery stable. He had two half-grown sons who hung around sometimes. The girl's name was Fortune.

When she came with a pitcher of lemonade (pretending she did not know Pete was away just then), Caleb said, "You don't look old enough to have boys as big as they are."

She answered, with a laugh, "They're not mine, except I'm raising them. I'm Pete's sister."

She was a pretty girl, calm and easy to talk to.

When Caleb was well enough, he moved to the hotel. But first he called on the local banker, made some arrangements, and paid the doctor. After that, the hotelkeeper was cordial, although Caleb wore the same clothes he had come in. They were clean now, and no longer ragged but nicely mended by Fortune. Even when Caleb lived at the hotel, he spent much time at the livery stable, talking to Pete or anybody, because he wasn't yet able to do anything else.

Pete asked no questions, but he was willing to answer them.

"How long you been here?" Caleb inquired, just passing time.

"Came right after the war. Some of my folks was here before me."

"I came by here once, to the old fort, with a wagon train on the way west," Caleb volunteered, hating to remember but having a need to mention it. "Things have changed."

And with me they've changed, he assured himself. *Gold banked with Wells Fargo now. I can have just about anything—but what do I want? Why, just to prove to somebody that was here once that I amount to something. A fool reason for heading this way, but a man's got to head somewhere.*

Pete's boys went into the house across the road, and Caleb asked lazily, "What makes the younger one limp?"

"Got hurt when he was a baby. Don't mention it to him—he hates that limp."

"How old is he?"

"Twelve. Wesley's fourteen. . . . What you shivering for? Got a chill?"

"Goose walked over my grave. I'm all right."

But they could be the same boys who had

howled with fear ten years ago. Fortune could be the little girl he remembered with envy and distaste, the little girl he wanted to prove something to and still wanted never to see again.

But they can't be, Caleb decided. *Those folks must have moved on.*

When he had been at the hotel for a week, he got up courage enough to ask if he might accompany Fortune to church.

"Why, I'd be pleased," she answered, looking as if she meant it. "There's preaching next Sunday. The circuit rider comes once a month."

"I figure to dress up a little better than I am now," Caleb promised.

"A person can go to church in whatever clothes they've got," Fortune said stoutly.

He bought new clothes and a black scarf to make a decent, inconspicuous sling for his left arm, which couldn't stand being moved much.

Sunday morning lasted about a month, he calculated, until it was time to call for Fortune at the house across from the livery stable.

Fortune's nephew Basil, who walked with a limp, said, "She ain't ready yet."

Fortune called from somewhere, "I am so!" but didn't come for a few minutes.

Basil and his brother, Wesley, had found Caleb in a field, facedown and bloody, with his horse

114

standing over him because he had tied the reins to his good arm before he fainted. They took it for granted he was dead, but Basil had dared to touch him so as to boast that he had touched a dead man. Basil was still a little edgy with Caleb because of that.

Fortune came into the kitchen, walking rapidly with small steps, neatly slim in a gray dress. She said, "Good morning, Caleb," in businesslike fashion.

He answered, "Good morning, Miss Fortune," and wished he hadn't, because she dimpled and young Basil haw-hawed. "I mean, Miss Wilson," he corrected, embarrassed. He had not called her anything before that day.

"You may call me by my first name," she said, "without any Miss on it."

Basil remarked, "She says it's a misfortune to be Miss Fortune."

"It is my good fortune to take her to church," replied Caleb, feeling better about everything.

This is a more important day, he thought, *than any day there ever was. More important than the day I found colors in the pan at Greasy Gulch or the day I sold my mine.*

And he thought—he hoped—it was important for her, too. She seemed breathless, as he was. It was a wonderful thing that had happened. One day he was a sick stranger lying in a stable, and another day he was almost well and Fortune was glad of his company.

My life is twisted with hers for good now, he realized. *Forever, even if we part forever. For no reason except that we have met and she likes me.*

In church she made sure nobody bumped his arm, and he wanted to protect her from dragons. But there were no dragons, unless you counted the inquisitive good women, and they attacked Caleb, not Fortune, with their questions.

"You're getting better, I see. Just how did it happen?"

"Three men dry-gulched me, ma'am, and thought they finished me off."

"At Greasy Gulch, we heard."

"A little this side of there, ma'am. I didn't aim to go back there and run into the same robbers, so I rode this way."

Ninety miles of pain and horror, of increasing fever and increasing fear that he wasn't going to make it.

"And Pete Wilson's boys found you. How fortunate!"

"Yes, ma'am. It was, indeed."

They eyed him closely, pretending not to. If he could wear good clothes now and stay at the hotel, why had he come in rags?

He had headed out of Greasy Gulch silently, by night, alone, but the road agents guessed it and ambushed him. They got maybe a hundred dollars in dust for their trouble. The rest of it had gone out on Wells Fargo's treasure coach and was safe. But all that was none of the good ladies' business.

"You were prospecting?" one of the women inquired.

"Lately I was mining, ma'am," he answered, and the woman didn't know the difference between seeking for gold and digging it out after you'd found where it was.

Someone asked, "Do you plan to stay here for a while?" but Fortune interrupted, saying that they'd have to go now to see whether the boys had put the potatoes on, as instructed. So he didn't have to answer that question.

On the way to the Wilson house, they were breathless again. "It's a lovely day, isn't it?" "A fine day, indeed." "Sun's bright but not too warm." "How pretty the light is on the cottonwoods!" "Sure is pretty." "Yes, it is." Being together was so splendid, so important, that they could not speak of anything that mattered.

The boys had put the potatoes on and kept the fire going. Fortune tied on a starched apron and busied herself with Sunday dinner, while Caleb

117

watched. Watching Fortune mash the potatoes was as fine a sight as he'd ever seen, he thought. As pretty as flake gold showing yellow in a pan of gravel.

Fortune told the boys, "Now, go get your father. We'll be ready soon as he washes up."

When Pete Wilson sat down with them at the table, he guessed the situation, and Caleb saw his face change, sag into weariness.

Fine way I'm treating the man who saved my life, Caleb thought. *He's got two motherless boys to raise, and now he figures to lose his sister that's raising them. Maybe on account of that, she wouldn't go away with me if I asked her. Fortune is a girl that wouldn't shirk her duty.*

But we needn't go away! he thought suddenly. *A man that's got fifteen thousand dollars put away with Wells Fargo can live anywhere.*

Caleb was so recently rich that the idea still shocked him. He hadn't yet got any pleasure out of it to speak of, except buying a fine chestnut horse in Greasy Gulch and now his new clothes.

"Shall I cut your meat, Caleb?" Fortune asked. "With your sore arm, you can't."

"You cooked it so tender it don't need a knife," he said, and she looked pleased.

"Wouldn't be interested in selling your horse," Fortune's brother suggested. "A man was in,

118

asking if it was for sale or not."

Caleb shook his head. "If you had a real good horse for the first time in your life, would you sell him?"

"Not if I didn't have to."

"I don't have to. I never had any luck till lately," Caleb explained. "Worked at one thing and another since I was a young kid. I struck pay dirt at Greasy Gulch. Enough so the road agents figured I was worth robbing."

Fortune was not startled at the news that he had found gold. She beamed approval, because she was sure that so remarkable a man as Caleb naturally would find what he was looking for.

Her brother commented, without jealousy, "Struck it rich. Well, I'm glad to hear it."

"And all the gold in the gulch wouldn't have helped me if you hadn't taken me in," Caleb reminded him. Then he made a mistake. He added, "I aim to pay you for what you did."

"No," Pete said, offended. "I make out all right with my business."

One of the boys yelled from the yard, "Hey, Pa, Mr. Hendrickson wants the sorrel."

Pete got up, grumbling, "He can't have it when it's out, can he?" and went across the road to his place of business.

So Caleb and Fortune were in the kitchen by

themselves, and Caleb longed to say something memorable, but Fortune became very housewifely just then.

"Just you sit," she advised, "while I pick up the dishes."

"Please," he said, "I'd like to help with them."

She glanced at his arm in its sling and answered, with the sweetest smile he had ever seen, "Some other time you can."

And he knew that she had said something memorable, even if he hadn't. It was a hint of a promise. There would be other times. He wanted to yell with jubilation, but he only smiled instead, and they understood each other perfectly.

"Smoke if you want to," Fortune invited, so he lighted a cigar and admired her domesticity.

There was a quick movement outside—he only glimpsed it, without understanding. But Fortune said, "I declare!" and ran out, dropping her dish towel. Caleb waited, puzzled, for it seemed to him that nothing had happened except that one of the boys had run past, and why should that upset her?

She mothers those kids, he thought. *She mothers everybody.*

He remembered a little girl of whom he had thought the same thing, a gaunt, serene child, who had once been near this fort.

120

It can't be the same, he told himself. They surely didn't stay. She had two little brothers—or were they her brothers? They could have been nephews. He hadn't been concerned with relationships that day ten years before, when he himself was fourteen.

He did not want Fortune to be that little girl grown-up. He remembered the time and the girl with horror. He was so disturbed that he got up and walked back and forth across the floor while he waited for Fortune to come back.

"What's wrong?" he demanded.

Something certainly was wrong. He thought she had been crying.

"It's Basil. Some new boys teased him because he's lame. It's a terrible thing; it happens too often. And he gets mad and cries, and that makes him madder."

"But you made him feel better."

She shook her head. "Not unless it helped him to take his mad out on me. He said it's my fault he's lame, and it is. I—I hurt him when he was two years old."

Then she was crying, with her hands over her face, and Caleb yearned toward her, wanting to touch her but aware that he had no right.

"It wasn't your fault," he insisted. "It couldn't have been. You wouldn't hurt anybody."

121

"But I broke his leg," she sobbed. "I should have managed better."

Caleb put his good hand on her arm firmly, whether he had any right or not.

"Look at me, Fortune, and stop crying." He knew now that she was that little girl he remembered. "Was it when the Indians came and you hid the children in a tree?" he demanded.

She gasped and stared at him, trembling. She didn't say yes. She didn't have to.

So Caleb would be no hero to Fortune now. He would kill no dragons for her. And all because he had been a coward when he was fourteen years old, and she had kept her head in the midst of danger—and remembered, when it was over with, to come and comfort him.

Caleb thought bleakly, *Well, I can partly pay Pete back. Pete's charity and mine can sort of balance out.*

"Call Basil in here," he commanded. "I want to tell him something. What have you been telling him all these years?"

"Why, what could I tell him? I never meant to hurt him, but I did, and he's lame for life."

There was, Caleb thought, a dragon he could kill for Basil, at least, and then he would ride on somewhere, away from the old fort that was called a settlement now. Maybe the truth would help

Fortune, too, but it would do no good for Caleb.

She didn't have to call the boy. He limped in and went to the kitchen pump for a drink.

"Go tell your pa I want a rig and a horse," Caleb ordered. "Mine's not broke to harness. You and I and Fortune are going for a drive."

"What for?" the boy challenged, snuffling.

"I want to show you a place and tell you what happened there." Caleb turned to Fortune. "How far is it? Ten, eleven miles?"

She was trembling. "I won't go. I've never been back there. I won't go."

"Yes, you'll go," he said gently, "because you have to."

She would not sit next to him in the buggy but put Basil between them. Caleb talked about the sun and the trees, but nobody answered.

It was a long drive to the place, and ten years since he had seen it, but he found the overgrown wagon road. He had gone that way on foot the other time—first, mile by slow mile, with the wagon train westward, and then alone, into a meadow, looking for a lost cow. He could have recognized now any landmark in the hundreds of miles he had trudged ten years before.

"We'll leave the horse here," he said when he found the old wagon track. "From here we'll walk the rest of the way."

Basil whined, "I don't want to. This is where the Indians came."

Caleb tied the horse to a tree. "Do you remember anything about it?"

The boy shook his head. "I was only two."

"Did you ever stop to think you're lucky not to remember it?" Caleb asked.

He led the way along the traces of a rough road.

I am fourteen years old, he thought, *and I am looking for Mr. Forsyth's cow. Not that his lost cow is any concern of mine, but I want the people in the wagon train to know how useful I am. Maybe some of them will take me in when we get to Idaho, because my sister Elsie is going to marry that man Hankins, and he doesn't like me. There'll be no place for me in their house when they get one.*

Fortune spoke piteously behind him, "Why do we have to go to—this place?"

"To see that it is only a little meadow with nothing in it. And to tell Basil some things he doesn't know."

There was no menace there. No menace had whispered the first time he walked that wagon track, either. But he had smelled smoke that other time and had seen the charred, ruined cabin and a dead man, bloody, lying on the ground.

Caleb turned to Fortune and asked, "Will you

tell your nephew what happened here, or shall I do it?"

She would not answer, except to shake her head.

"All right. I will, as far I can. Basil, see that old broken snag to the right of the cabin? She hid inside that snag with you boys. There's a window at the back of the cabin. You can't see it from here. I guess she went out that window while the Indians were busy with the man out in front.

"I never found out who he was," Caleb said, feeling faintly surprised. "I never asked." Or cared, either, he admitted to himself. The man was dead and didn't matter.

Fortune said in a strained voice, "My father's brother. He went out, and they killed him. It gave me time to go out the back window with the boys."

She looked at the ground before her feet, but she did not turn her back on the place of horror.

"She could have run and saved herself," Caleb told the boy. "But she took the two of you out with her, and she put you both in that hollow snag before she climbed in to hide. Remember that, boy. When the Indians were killing a man, not twenty feet away, she didn't run and save herself and leave you. And she wasn't more than twelve years old, I judge."

Basil's head was bent, but he kept stealing glances at the ruined cabin and the hollow snag, crumbling now with rot.

I've given him something to think about, Caleb told himself. *Something nobody bothered about before. They never talked about all this any more than they had to. It was something they would rather not think about at all.*

Basil demanded, "And where were you?"

"Way on beyond by the river with a wagon train when this happened. Nobody knew it was happening. We were stopped for Sunday by the river, so the women could do their washing and we could go on to the fort next day. I was traveling with my older sister and her kids. I came this way on foot, looking for a lost cow.

"First I smelled smoke. Then I saw the meadow with the cabin in it. And a man lying there."

Basil was seeing those things, too, identifying himself with that other boy, who had become a man named Caleb Stark.

Basil asked in a hushed voice, "Why didn't you run?"

"Why, because—" *Why didn't I?* Caleb wondered. "I guess because I didn't believe it, what I was seeing. The meadow was so quiet, so peaceful; not even a bee buzzing. It was as quiet as— death. You know," he said earnestly, "you can't believe death, either, first time you see it close."

The boy blinked. "Like I saw you lying in the

field. I thought you were dead."

"And you touched me so you could boast you had touched a dead man. You didn't want to. You were afraid. But you did it. It didn't matter one way or another. Except then you saw the dead man was breathing, and went for your pa."

Basil nodded, feeling himself something of a hero.

"It was something like that with me, here at the edge of the meadow. After I could believe what had happened, then I was scared. I wanted to run; I was going to run and get out of here. But there was a little sound from over to the right there, a faint little sound in the deathly quiet. I thought it was a wounded Indian, and I thought if he was wounded I could kill him—and have something to boast about back at the wagon camp.

"Because, Lord knows," Caleb burst out, "I never had had anything to boast about or be proud of, and it was time I did. So I yelled something, some kind of challenge. I don't know what it was."

Fortune spoke quietly. "You said, 'Damn you, I'll shoot!' and I couldn't hold my hand over Basil's mouth any longer, because he'd bitten me, and he screamed, and then you came and got us out of the hollow snag."

Caleb said to the boy, "How many hours did she stay in there, cramped in there with you two kids, holding your mouths so you couldn't scream and bring the Indians back to kill the lot of you? She was so cramped she couldn't climb out.

"I found an ax with the handle half burned off and had to chop out the side of the snag before any of you could get out. I was so scared I couldn't even see good. It's a wonder I didn't chop you with that ax."

He felt bathed with shame, as always, remembering how scared he had been, how witless. And how cool and sensible that little girl was, telling him what to do as she lay on the ground where she had fallen out of the snag. She was trying to move her cramped legs, and her face was contorted with the pain, but she wasn't crying; she never cried once. And she thought of everything.

Caleb went on. "First thing she said was, 'Get the kids some water.' I didn't want to stop for that. I wanted to get out of this place to where it was safer. But she said, 'Get the kids some water,' and told me where the spring was, so I carried water in my hat, and she didn't drink till after you boys did."

Every step of the way, he remembered silently, *I hated her for delaying me. I hunched my muscles, expecting a bullet from somewhere in the brush, or an Indian yell with death right behind it.*

"And I wanted to go then, just grab one of you

129

kids and run for it—or leave you there, for that matter. I didn't care. But she said, 'Basil's hurt,' and I saw your leg looked crooked. You were trying to crawl but you couldn't, and you and your brother were howling blue murder. I thought you'd bring the Indians, for sure.

"She said, 'You'll have to brace his leg someway to carry him. Get a stick or something to tie to it.' She thought of that, even, and told me, while she was still working the cramps out of her legs. So I got a straight stick and then couldn't think of anything to tie it with, but she tore the shirt off your brother, and we tied the splint that way. She got blood on the cloth, because you'd bitten that deep into her hand.

"When she could walk, she dragged your brother by the hand, and I carried you and my rifle, and we went as fast as we could along the wagon track to get out of here."

Fortune whispered, "Then we had to hide."

That was another thing that Caleb hated to remember—and to have her remember.

"I was so scared," he said slowly. "We heard men's voices ahead of us on the wagon track, and I couldn't move anymore. I was so big a coward that I couldn't move or think. I just stood there, hanging on to you and waiting to be killed."

Fortune said sharply, "Nonsense! I was the

scared one. I said, 'Let's hide,' and we did, in the brush. But it wasn't Indians; it was men from the wagons."

"I was a coward," Caleb repeated. "But after that it didn't matter much, because they hustled us out of there.

"That's all, kid. You can be glad you don't remember anything about it."

Caleb turned abruptly and led the way back along the grass-grown ruts, away from the quiet meadow where death and terror had been a long time ago.

On the way back to the old fort, Fortune was willing to sit beside him in the rig, with her hands in her lap. After a while she said, "That wasn't all. You gave me your coat. And I think it was the only one you had."

Caleb shrugged. "My sister fixed me another one."

He remembered that makeshift coat with shame. It was made of a torn patchwork quilt. He wore it when he had to, the rest of the way to Idaho, and many a time he shivered in the cold rather than to put it on. Some of the people laughed, and some tried to comfort him, which was worse. They called it Caleb's coat of many colors; they said the lilies of the field were not arrayed like Caleb.

I've got fifteen thousand dollars banked with Wells Fargo, he reminded himself. But that did not erase the bitter memory of the gaudy coat that took the place of the one he gave away.

Fortune said suddenly, "Basil, he didn't tell you the straight of it. That boy that rescued us—I never knew his name till today—he was no coward. He was the bravest boy I ever knew. He could have run away. Nobody would have known. Nobody but him, anyway. But he stayed and got us out.

"Some people took us in their wagon for overnight, and a man who did some doctoring fixed your leg as well as he could, and they fed us. My father was coming from the fort; we met him on the way. He and Uncle Will used to sell hay there. That's why we were at the meadow.

"Just before the wagon train moved on to the fort, Caleb saw I was cold, and he gave me his coat.

"I still have it."

Caleb said, "What!"

"I wore it out, because we didn't have much in those days. But I've still got it, what there is left. It was something—to remember you by."

Caleb said gently, "Why, Fortune!"

And then nobody said anything the rest of the way to the settlement that had once been a fort.

That chilly morning long ago, cold before the

sun came up, he wore his ragged brown coat while he harnessed the horses. The whole camp was stirring, getting ready to move on, and he felt that everybody stared at him. He was no hero; he was only an unwanted boy who had brought in some other unwanted, desperate children that somebody had to look after, at least temporarily.

The people felt that he had just about brought the Indians down on them. Men had been on guard all night, and nobody got much sleep.

Mr. Forsyth slouched up to him and said, with a long face, "I don't suppose you found my cow."

"Never saw her," Caleb admitted.

Forsyth sighed and slouched away, not saying, "Thanks for your trouble," just giving the impression that nobody expected Caleb to succeed even at a simple thing like that.

Caleb wondered, as he worked, what he would do in Idaho. There would be no place for him in his sister's home, and Caleb had a poor opinion of his own abilities. No one had ever suggested that he had any abilities. He was small for his age, hadn't got his growth, and that would handicap him in getting work.

He was as miserable as he had ever been in his life when the little girl came to him from behind a wagon. Her face was clean, and her hair was combed and braided, but she wore the same stained, torn dress, and she shivered, hugging herself with her arms but not saying anything about being cold. Someone had tied a clean rag on her hand, the hand the baby had bitten.

Caleb looked at her with distaste. The people in the wagons blamed him because they were worried about Indians. He had nobody to blame but the girl whose name he didn't know and didn't want to know.

She said politely, "I wanted to say thank you."

He shrugged, not knowing any better answer. He detested her, because her need was so great and her future so bleak, and she wasn't afraid of anything.

In the growing light of dawn, she stepped toward him. Before he could guess her intention, she took his scowling face between her hands and lightly kissed his cheek.

He jumped back, angrily scrubbing at his face, and demanded, "What's that for?"

"I don't know," she said and turned away.

That was when he couldn't stand her shivering anymore. He shucked off his old brown coat and threw it at her.

"Put that on," he growled.

She nodded and kept on walking away while she thrust her thin arms into the sleeves.

"I'll show you!" he muttered. "I'll come back

sometime and show you!"

Show her what? Why, that he amounted to something, even if she didn't think so, even if she had come and kissed him, as if he were a baby to be pitied.

In the settlement that was a fort no longer, Caleb pulled up in front of the Wilson house. He helped Fortune down and ordered, "Basil, take the outfit back to your pa."

Then he stood looking into Fortune's quiet face.

"Why," he asked, "did you kiss me long ago?"

"It was all I had to give you," she replied. "Like the coat was all you had to give me."

Caleb nodded. He should have understood that all along.

"The years gone by were bad ones," he said. "The years to come will be better."

He was almost sure of that, but he was completely certain when she put both her hands into his outstretched hand and answered, "Why, yes, Caleb. Of course they will."

Blessed Event

Mary Sellars

THERE'S CLYTIE at the back door now," said Betsey, pulling herself up from the cushions as the mewing became continuous and insistent. She was talking to herself; she was alone in the house. Both Father and Mother were at the firm's banquet, and her young brother, Buff, was spending the night with his best friend, Joey.

Betsey was still undecided what to do, but she had agreed not to go out until Clytie was safely indoors, at any rate. She could still call Rosemary and invite her over to make fudge or something, but there was a new murder mystery from the lending library, and she had become absorbed in it as she ate her supper on a tray, comfortably sprawled on the sofa. It was good; really terrific, in fact. She had half a mind to curl up with it for the rest of the evening and forget Rosemary.

Clytie streaked past her as she opened the door, looking bleak and chilly; there was a sprinkle of drizzle on her fur. The drizzle settled it. Rosemary would try to talk *her* into walking the six blocks instead. No; she and Clytie and *The Corpse with the Seven Fingers* would spend a nice, cozy evening together.

"Here's your supper," called Betsey, putting down a dish under the stove. But Clytie just stood and looked at it briefly, then rejected it, with an expression of such complete loathing that it was almost human. She trotted ahead of Betsey into the living room, where she burrowed into the corduroy cushion of her favorite chair and began to lick herself dry of raindrops.

Oh, dear, she must be having one of her queer spells tonight, thought Betsey, settling back on the sofa once more.

Then, as she had often done recently, Betsey laid the book on her chest and studied Clytie. She was going to have kittens fairly soon, and she looked so thin and vulnerable to be carrying that burden. It was her first litter; she was still a young cat, hardly grown-up, really—not one of those plump, matronly tabbies.

I wonder what she's thinking, mused Betsey. *I*

*wonder if she knows what's happening to her,
what's going to happen; really knows, I mean—not
just a vague instinct to look for a nest. I wonder if
she's scared.*

The way I would be, she might have added, only
she wouldn't let herself even think the words.

She had known about how babies were born
for quite a long time now, of course, and all the
books she had been given to read had been thoroughly sensible and cheerful about it. But it wasn't
so much the things you read; it was the things you
heard. Things you heard from other girls, for in-
stance—from somebody who'd had it from somebody who'd had it from somebody who had a married sister or cousin. That sort of thing. Or the
frightening possibilities you could imagine from
phrases, half sentences you overheard in a bus or
a movie queue. Looking up words you didn't know
before, not knowing whether half the things re-
ferred to happened to everybody or just a few
isolated cases. You brooded and wished you were
a boy and thought how unfair it was.

Betsey could remember the time when she was
a good deal younger and had said worriedly to
Mother, "They say it hurts more than anything in
the world."

One part of Betsey had wished then that her
mother would deny it categorically, say something

brisk and cheerful like "Nonsense! Why, it's nothing at all!" Not that Betsey would have believed her, but in some obscure way it would have relieved her. But Mother had tried to be honest and at the same time reassuring.

"Oh, I wouldn't say that," she had said, choosing her words carefully. "It's—well, it's a bit of an ordeal, certainly, but, you know, afterward, mothers are so happy about having their babies they forget all about it right away."

It had been haunting Betsey for ages. *Oh, not all the time, by any means—after all, I'm not a goon,* she told herself hastily. Only, when the subject happened to come up, it was hard to shake it off afterward. She read every article on medical developments she could find, but it didn't clear things up much. It was just confusing. It seemed there were drugs that made everything easy. If only one knew for sure. . . .

Of course, people said it was worth it, anyway. But was it? Was anything worth it? It wasn't that she didn't like babies; she did—and naturally, she thought, you wanted to be married and have a family; but sometimes she wondered how you could so lightheartedly get married, as older girls seemed to be doing all the time, when there would be *this* hanging over you.

I won't think about it, she told herself firmly.

139

I don't know why I ever let myself get started. I've got a nice, cheerful murder mystery to take my mind off it. She reached for a bowl of walnuts and the nutcracker and settled back once more.

"Clytie, must you pace up and down like that?" she asked about half an hour later. "It's very distracting."

But Clytie only looked at her accusingly and continued to pace.

"I expect you're cold. It is a bit damp and chilly tonight. Here, I'll light the fire for you."

Betsey touched a match to the kindling, and in a minute a cheerful blaze was flickering around the logs. Clytie moved gratefully into the glow and toasted her face; she loved a fire. Betsey went back to her book.

But the peace did not last long. With her tail thrashing restlessly, Clytie took up her march again, and a strange, complaining noise came from the back of her throat. She came over and stood looking up at Betsey piteously.

"Waa-aa," she wailed suddenly, in a self-pitying voice so unlike the truculent "Wow!" with which she usually demanded attention.

"Poor Clytie! Is this one of your bad days, darling?" murmured Betsey soothingly. "Here, come up beside me, and I'll pet you."

Clytie came, but there was no soothing her. She

did not rub her head against Betsey's hand or respond at all to the stroking. Instead, she walked up and down all over Betsey, still making the lugubrious, complaining noise. Then she would sit down and cling desperately, staring into her face; her claws dug through the tweed skirt as she flexed and unflexed them. Clytie, it was clear, was hating the way she was feeling and was obviously scared stiff.

The horror of a suspicion flashed into Betsey's mind.

"Oh, no, Clytie!" she whispered, aghast. "You can't do this to me. Not when I'm alone in the house. You just can't!"

But Clytie was already moving in the direction of the cellar door; she had picked out her maternity ward some time ago, choosing, of all places, the shower stall in the basement. So the family had resigned themselves to tub baths for a while, and Betsey's mother had fixed up a comfortable bed there, all ready for her. Now, as Clytie started down the stairs, she made it very clear by her pauses, her backward glances, and her pleading wails, that she intended Betsey to follow her. Clytie wanted to have her hand held; there was no getting away from it.

What on earth am I supposed to do? thought Betsey desperately. *I suppose if I'd been brought up on a farm, this sort of thing would be all in the day's work. But I wasn't. And I don't even want to be there. Very definitely, I don't.*

As far as she could recall, their other cats had been experienced and capable. They had simply disappeared conveniently and reappeared the next day, proudly displaying their latest batch of infants. Either that, or Mother had coped.

Only I can't *call Mother away from a banquet,* she told herself, *especially when it's twenty-five miles away.* There was Mrs. Jergens, of course, and Rosemary would certainly rally round in an emergency. But Clytie had been as nervous as a gazelle about strangers recently; she wouldn't let anyone but the family near her. If visitors even spoke to her, she shot out of the room and wouldn't come back till they had gone. No, it would be mean to upset her now.

Well, it had to be done, she decided resolutely, although her mouth was dry, and the butterflies were apparently holding a square dance in her stomach. She couldn't let Clytie down. So she pulled up a box to sit on at the door of the shower, and she stroked Clytie's head gently and made reassuring noises. "Only I hope it won't be long," she whispered. "Please don't let it be long."

Time seemed to stand still as she sat there stiffly, only moving to shift her feet a fraction of an inch on the rough concrete floor. It was as if she and Clytie were alone somewhere, cut off from the world, at the bottom of the sea, perhaps, fighting something out together. Upstairs, the phone shrilled, seven interminable times. She ignored it, but it seemed to increase the feeling of isolation.

But at least Clytie wasn't terrified anymore. She realized she wasn't going to be alone, and by now she had recognized the situation for what it was. Instinct had taken over. Periodically the wails started up again, and they harrowed Betsey's soul.

After what seemed like hours, Betsey shifted her numbed muscles and peeked at her watch. Actually, it had been less than forty minutes. Incredible. The box was uncomfortable, her right foot was asleep, and there was a fearful draft on the floor. But she knew she would stick it out with Clytie. In the end she decided to close her eyes; somehow it didn't seem considerate to stare, and, besides, she didn't want to.

When she opened them again, the first kitten—unbelievably tiny and fragile—had been born, and Clytie was licking it furiously, as if its very life depended on it.

And in a way it did, Betsey discovered a moment later. For as soon as she had finished, Clytie began to nudge and bump the little thing with her nose, rolling it over and over in a way that seemed awfully drastic until it dawned on Betsey what she was doing. Of course. It wasn't really alive yet. Clytie was trying to make it squeal, so that it would open its mouth and start breathing. And even as she realized it, there was a protesting yelp, and a tiny pink tongue appeared. There it was, a brand-new, living kitten.

Betsey gazed and gazed at it as it fumbled helplessly around on the blanket. It was so incredibly small, hardly two inches long, dappled gray, like Clytie, with a face like a tiny, blurred pansy. Just a blind, helpless smudge of fur, but complete in miniature, and somehow the most wonderful, touching thing she had ever seen in her life.

There were three kittens born, altogether; the second one was dappled black, with an absurd white nose, and the third a lighter gray. But something awful happened when the third one was launched.

Clytie pushed and bumped it around, rolled it over, just as she had the other two. Only this time there was no response. She tried again. Still nothing happened; the kitten lay inert. Then, to Betsey's utter dismay, Clytie simply abandoned it and busied herself with the other two, who were still mewing plaintively. She had gone as far as instinct directed her and then stopped; that was as much as she knew.

145

"Oh, Clytie," whispered Betsey, "you can't just let it go like that. *You can't.*" By tipping an edge of the blanket, she pushed the kitten gently toward her, but Clytie would not see it. She was deeply absorbed in getting the others to nurse.

Something had to be done. For some reason Betsey could not have explained, it was terribly important that the kitten should live. It would spoil everything, all the joy and satisfaction, if they were left, in the end, with that pitiful, lifeless little thing.

She bent down and very tentatively stretched out her hand toward it, looking questioningly at Clytie to see if she minded. But it was all right. She was her pal; Clytie trusted her completely. So, very gingerly and trembling, Betsey picked up the kitten, put it in the palm of one hand, and spanked it with the tip of her index finger. Nothing happened. On a sudden inspiration, she reached for her handkerchief and with a corner of it carefully wiped the minute nose, in case the breathing passages were blocked. Then she poked it again and rolled it over the way Clytie had done. It was no use; it wouldn't mew. It lay warm and limp on her hand.

Beads of perspiration stood on Betsey's forehead. Everything else was blotted from her mind except the urgency of saving the kitten. No practical considerations even entered her head. Not once did she think, *What's one kitten more or less?* You couldn't look at it and think that. You couldn't.

Well—evidently sterner measures were necessary. Betsey pulled back her middle finger with her thumb. Then, gritting her teeth because it seemed like the cruelest thing she had ever done, she administered a really stinging flick to its midriff. The small pink mouth opened at last.

"Wai-ai-ai," yelled the outraged kitten.

It was alive.

Clytie looked up at the sound and stared interestedly at Betsey's hand, but just for a minute Betsey kept the kitten, feeling the warm palpitation of its breathing against her palm. All her fear was gone. She felt a tremendous surge of pride, a glow. *It's alive,* she thought wonderingly, *and I did it. Doctors must feel like that, only much more so. It's amazing. There's really nothing quite like it.*

Finally she laid the kitten down. Clytie looked at it curiously for a moment, then accepted it. All the same, she gave it a thorough going over with her tongue, just to make it one of the family.

Betsey went upstairs and fetched some warm milk, but Clytie was too occupied right then to bother with it.

"I'll just leave it here, then, where you can

reach it," she told Clytie, making a safe place for it beside the bed.

Then she stood up and was engulfed in an enormous yawn of sheer exhaustion. For the first time in two hours, she could relax. She stretched luxuriously and massaged her feet, which were like ice blocks. Then she looked at Clytie, and she had to chuckle.

"Oh, Clytie!" she said weakly. "*Honestly—*"

For there was no doubt who had come out of this the best. Every muscle in Betsey's body ached with tension, her palms were clammy, and her hair and the collar of her blouse clung damply to her neck. She felt utterly limp. "I'm just a wreck," she told the cat severely.

But Clytie—Clytie looked as if she had just won a queen-for-a-day contest. There was not a sign, now, of the thin, frightened, miserable creature of two hours ago. One of the kittens was nursing; the other two were asleep; and Clytie lay, circling them, completely relaxed but with her head held proud and high. Every hair of her coat seemed to have taken on a new, sleek luster. She no longer looked young and anxious, even; she was a serene, completely satisfied matron-cat.

And you know, thought Betsey, *she doesn't look as if she'd just been through a lot of pain. It's more as though she'd just struggled awfully hard to*

148

accomplish something and had succeeded.

Certainly Clytie looked supremely happy and almost indecently pleased with herself. The whole basement throbbed with the noise of her purring, steady and strong, like a turbine.

"So you do forget," said Betsey softly, looking down at them, "and it all seems absolutely worthwhile. I'm glad I know."

She bent down and touched *her* kitten lightly with one finger. "You're special," she said. "I'm going to see if Mother will let us keep you."

Suddenly she felt marvelous, absolutely terrific.

"I guess you don't need me for a while," she said to Clytie. "I'll see you later. You can turn your nose up at milk if you like, but I'm *hungry*."

She raced up the basement stairs.

A Christmas Tradition

Lorena K. Sample

CAROLE LAUGHED delightedly. "I've never seen anything like it. A whole forest of Christmas trees! How can you ever decide which one to cut?"

Gary Matthews grinned at her enthusiasm. "Granddad wouldn't think of cutting any of these scrawny little trees. Wait until we get to the other side of the hill."

Carole dropped to a snow-capped stump to rest and catch her breath. Ahead of them marched Gary's grandfather, saw in hand. On either side ranged children of assorted ages, busily hurling snowballs, climbing trees, making angel shapes in the snow. Back at the parked cars, far down the hill, people moved to and fro around the bonfire. They looked almost like dancers, their music the children's yells and laughter.

"You do this every year?" Carole asked wistfully. "The whole family gets together and comes out here to cut a tree?"

"A family tradition. Granddad cuts the biggest and best tree for the farm, and then each family cuts a smaller one for its own home," Gary explained. "We take most of the presents to Granddad's to open Christmas morning, and then we have turkey dinner there."

With her mittened hand, Carole drew a fat Santa in the powdery snow. "We don't have any family traditions," she said slowly. "Sometimes we open our presents Christmas Day and sometimes Christmas Eve. We may have scrambled eggs or TV dinners, or we may eat out. Last year we didn't even have a Christmas tree."

"Well, I suppose it's pretty hard to do the same thing every year, when you move around so much," Gary said. "You were in Florida last year, weren't you? Couldn't you get a tree?"

"We hadn't anyplace to put one. We had two Cuban refugee families living with us, and the living room was full of sleeping bags for the kids," Carole explained. She squinted in the glare from the glistening snow, remembering other years. "The year before, when we were in Minnesota, one of the men on Dad's construction crew had a fire in his trailer house, and we gave all our Christmas presents to his family. The year before that, Melody found a kitten with a Christmas ribbon around its neck, and our dinner burned while we ran around trying to find out if the kitten was supposed to be a Christmas surprise for some little child. And the year before *that*—"

Gary held up a hand and grinned. "I'm convinced. Christmas is just one more day of mass confusion in the Brody household. But sometimes traditions do just get to be a lot of bother."

Carole shook her head vehemently. "I don't think I'd ever, *ever* get tired of doing something traditional every year." She stood up and brushed the snow off her blue ski pants.

They trooped over the hill and watched Gary's grandfather cut down a magnificent, full-branched fir, so lovely that Carole thought it scarcely needed decorations. Gary offered to cut a tree for her, but she thanked him and explained that her father had said he had his eye on a big one at a lot downtown. After they hiked back to the fire, she joined in the fun of roasting wieners over the fire. She was never treated as an outsider, though she'd been dating Gary only a short time.

"It was a wonderful day, Gary," Carole told him sincerely when he took her home. She began to

straighten the evergreen wreath she had made for the front door, the only Christmas decoration their home had.

"I'm glad you liked it. I was afraid— Well, you've lived everywhere and done so many things. I was afraid you might think the Matthews family ceremony of cutting the Christmas tree was just kind of silly."

"I don't think it's silly at all. I think it's a—a beautiful tradition," Carole said softly and then hurried inside.

Carole glanced around the living room, hoping her father might have brought the tree home from the lot, but there was no tree.

Nor was there a tree the following day or the day after that. Christmas was not wholly lost on her family, Carole thought, but it was certainly misplaced. Her younger sister, Melody, hummed Christmas carols one moment and wished she could go surfing the next. Mrs. Brody helped to decorate the tree in the children's wing at the hospital but seemed not at all concerned about the lack of decorations at home. Mr. Brody saw that the men on his construction crew each got a Christmas turkey but brought none home for the family.

Carole did not see as much of Gary as she had before the Christmas season, but he stopped by early in the afternoon on the day before Christmas.

"We always burn pine cones in the fireplace on Christmas," he explained. "Would you like to collect pine cones with me?"

He waited while she slipped into warm clothes, and then they drove south to a cousin's property near the river, where the snow was shallower than it was in the hills.

"This is one of our more recent traditions," Gary explained. "Sort of an accident, really. My uncle forgot to chop the wood he was supposed to one year. He gathered up a bunch of cones at the last minute, and everyone liked them so much that now we have to have cones every year."

"You know, I never thought about traditions having to *start* sometime. Maybe that's what's wrong with my family—no one ever started a tradition," Carole said thoughtfully. Her eyes sparkled. "I think I'll start a tradition!"

"You will?"

"It has to be something not too complicated, something fun. . . ."

"Do you have a tree yet? We could cut one."

Carole shook her head. "We might never live in another place where we could cut our own tree. It has to be something we can do every year. Something simple, like waiting until the day before Christmas to buy a tree, decorating it together

155

Christmas Eve, and then opening presents together Christmas morning."

After they had filled two cardboard boxes with
cones, Gary drove Carole around to half a dozen
Christmas tree lots. Only the scrawniest and least
shapely trees remained, but an attendant gave her
some extra branches to go with a medium-sized
fir. At the house, Gary carried the tree to the front
door for her.

"I'll try to come over sometime tomorrow," he
said, "if I can ever get away from the family.
Okay?"

Carole nodded happily, anxious to get inside
and get a tradition started.

"A tree!" Melody squealed.

Mr. Brody glanced up from his paper. "I guess
I forgot to get one. That one looks very nice," he
said approvingly.

Carole perched the tree in a corner. "Mom,
could you come in here a minute? I have a suggestion to make, and I'd like everyone to hear it."

Mrs. Brody came in from the kitchen, wiping
her hands, and Carole outlined her plan.

"Gary was right when he said Christmas was
just one more day of mass confusion around our
house," she concluded. "We need a tradition."

"I think Gary put it a bit harshly," Mrs. Brody
said mildly, "but getting a tradition started really

does sound like a marvelous idea."

"I think so, too," Melody agreed. "Only. . . ."

"What?"

"Well, I've already opened the present Aunt Cora sent. See?" Melody jangled the bracelet on her arm.

"But we'll keep all the other presents until tomorrow morning. Okay?" Carole asked.

"Agreed," Mrs. Brody said. "And now supper is ready. We can start decorating after we eat."

Carole wondered momentarily how many other Clarkstown families were eating enchiladas on Christmas Eve, but she decided not to dwell on trivialities. Perhaps next year they could add another tradition—something about a special Christmas Eve dinner.

While Carole and Melody did dishes, Mrs. Brody rummaged around looking for Christmas decorations. She finally returned with a string of lights and three red balls.

"These are all I can find. The other decorations must have been in some of the boxes of stuff I gave away when we left Florida."

"I'll run downtown and see if I can find a store that's still open. We can't let tradition get bogged down by a little thing like missing decorations," Mr. Brody said cheerfully. He squeezed Carole's shoulder as he left.

They draped the string of lights around the tree while he was gone, and Carole tied the extra branches in place to give the tree more shape and fullness. When Mr. Brody returned, he tossed the sack of decorations to Carole.

"Hey, guess who I just ran into," he said. "Harry Oersted. He invited us to go caroling with them. In a horse-drawn wagon!"

"Really?" Mrs. Brody asked excitedly. "You mean actually to ride around and sing Christmas songs to anyone who wants to listen?"

"Just like the pictures on Christmas cards!" Melody cut in. "Am I invited, too?"

Mrs. Brody glanced suddenly at Carole still standing in the center of the room with the unopened sack. "You wouldn't mind if we went, would you, hon? I've never been honest-to-goodness caroling. Why don't you come, too?"

Carole set the sack carefully beneath the tree. "No, I won't mind. You go ahead and go."

Melody dashed off, and Mrs. Brody followed her, like another teen-ager.

"What do you wear caroling?" Mrs. Brody asked. "Oh, dear, I'll freeze to death. Phil, did you *possibly* get me those black ski pants from Gillman?"

Mr. Brody chuckled. "After all those hints, what else could I get you?"

Carole heard the tearing of paper and the delighted squeals as Mrs. Brody unwrapped the new ski pants.

She tinkered halfheartedly with the Christmas decorations after the family had gone, but it was difficult carrying on a tradition alone, especially such a newborn tradition. She went to bed long before the others returned home.

She was also up before anyone else the next morning and was munching a piece of toast when Mrs. Brody entered the kitchen.

"Good morning." Carole hadn't especially meant her greeting to sound so cool, but it came out that way.

"Oh, hon, you're hurt about last night, aren't you? I'm so sorry. . . . It was just that caroling sounded like so much fun and so Christmasy." Mrs. Brody paused, as if searching for some further way to apologize. "How will it be if we run out and buy a turkey? I'll fix a great big turkey dinner, with all the trimmings."

"You can't get much more traditional than that, can you?" Mr. Brody asked, pushing through the swinging door into the kitchen. "Get Melody up, and we'll all go. Maybe we can make it a tradition that we all go together and buy a turkey on Christmas Day."

Carole blinked back tears of disappointment,

159

realizing that her parents were honestly trying to make it up to her. And besides, she comforted herself, a tradition of having a big turkey dinner for Christmas was better than no tradition at all.

Carole's spirits rose almost in spite of herself as they piled into the car in search of a market open on Christmas. It had snowed lightly during the night, and even the power lines and bare trees had lost their ugliness under the magic frosting.

"Now, we must not get a frozen one," Mrs. Brody cautioned as they finally located a little store with an OPEN sign hung on its door. "Remember the year we had Fourth of July dinner a day late because I didn't realize how long it takes a frozen turkey to defrost?"

Carole's lips curved in an unplanned smile. Who else had turkey for Fourth of July? Mrs. Brody was apt to cook turkey—or anything else—when the mood moved her.

The market had only one unfrozen bird remaining, a huge creature that Mrs. Brody eyed doubtfully.

"We'll be eating turkey leftovers for a month."

"Let's invite someone to dinner," Mr. Brody suggested.

"Oh, I don't think so," Carole said quickly. "I mean, people in Clarkstown all eat Christmas dinner with the same people, year after year." She didn't know quite how to explain that in Clarkstown you just didn't invite people over on the spur of the moment for Christmas dinner.

"That's silly," Melody scoffed. "There must be *someone* who'd like to eat with us."

They bought the turkey, and Mr. Brody suggested they drive around by the home of some people named Maley, who he thought might be having a skimpy Christmas.

Half a dozen cars were parked around the Maleys' home, and their Christmas looked anything but skimpy. There was no one home at the Dorins', whom Mrs. Brody suggested next. Carole felt foolish, running around searching for guests on Christmas Day, but the others seemed to regard each defeat as an added challenge.

"I know—Mac Davidson!" Mr. Brody said suddenly. "The company laid him off about a month ago, and his wife is in the hospital with a new baby. They have three boys, and I'll bet Mac would be delighted to be asked out for dinner."

The Davidsons' house was a square frame building, surrounded by vacant lots, on the outskirts of town. The snow around it had already been trampled to brown slush.

"Three boys—wow!" Melody said. "Maybe one of them is old enough for me." She scooted out of the car, and Carole followed less enthusiastically behind the other members of the family.

Just then Melody squealed, and an angry man waving a mop shot around the corner of the house.

"Get the dog! Get our turkey!"

"He's running under the car," Melody yelled. "We'll corner him!"

Reluctantly Carole knelt and peered beneath the car, just in time to be confronted by a strange-looking creature, half naked bird, half skinny, spotted dog. Spurred on by pursuers from behind, the creature chose Carole as his most harmless-looking adversary and tried to charge past her.

He succeeded not only in getting by her but also in sending her sprawling backward into the dirty snow and leaving a trail of muddy footprints across her shoulder.

"I'll get him!" Mr. Brody made a flying tackle—and missed. He skidded facedown across the slushy yard, and the dog raced off up the street with his prize.

Melody held her sides and gasped for breath through her laughter. "You two are forty years too late. You belong in silent slapstick movies!"

Mrs. Brody was more subtle, but her mouth twitched suspiciously as she tried to wipe the muddy splotches off Carole's jacket and skirt. By that time the three small Davidson boys had con-

gregated outside, and Mr. Davidson was trying to
apologize to Carole's father.

"Janie's coming home from the hospital with
the new baby this evening, and the boys and I
were going to surprise her by fixing Christmas dinner for her. And then Bobby brought home that
stray dog, and first thing I knew, there went dog
and turkey out the back door while I was mopping
up the milk Ryan had spilled." He glanced up the
street, as if hopeful that the dog might somehow
decide to return with their dinner. Carole remembered her father's saying Mr. Davidson had been
laid off work; there undoubtedly was not another
turkey in the Davidson budget.

"I think his cooking dinner was a sweet idea,"
Melody whispered. "It won't be the same, bringing her from the hospital to our place for dinner. I'll bet he had candlelight and everything
planned."

Carole couldn't quite imagine Mr. Davidson by
candlelight, but she supposed Mrs. Davidson
could, and somehow Carole knew what was coming. She could almost hear the wheels turning in
her father's head as he sorted and rejected ideas
while small-talking with Mr. Davidson.

Suddenly Mrs. Brody winked at the girls,
opened the car door, and pulled out the turkey.

"My husband seems to have forgotten why we

stopped by here in the first place," she said to Mr. Davidson. "We're a bit late getting the Christmas turkeys from the company delivered, but perhaps you'll still be able to use it."

"That one's a lot bigger'n the one we had!" one of the boys exclaimed.

Mr. Davidson thanked them and the company over and over again, until Carole's mother reminded him that he had better get it roasting if he wanted it done in time for Janie's homecoming.

By the time they backed out of the driveway, Carole's damp spots had soaked clear through to her skin in several places.

"Well, anyway, the poor dog looked as if he needed a Christmas dinner, too," Mr. Brody said philosophically.

"One more tradition down the drain," Melody added cheerfully.

"Oh, maybe we can find another store and get another turkey," Mrs. Brody protested, "although it would make dinner a little late now. . . ."

"A *little* late?" Melody groaned. "I shall positively starve if I don't get something to eat in the next fifteen minutes."

"How about eating out?" Mr. Brody suggested.

"Like this?" Carole pointed to her father's stained clothes and the damp blotches on her own.

"There's a drive-in in the next block," Mrs.

Brody said. "We could stop there."

Mr. Brody turned in at the drive-in, and the girl handed them menus. Mrs. Brody turned around and reached her hand into the backseat toward Carole.

"Hon, I really am sorry. Maybe next year. . . ."

Carole tried to smile, but somehow she knew next year would be no different from this year. There might or might not be a Christmas tree. They might have scrambled eggs or TV dinners, or they might eat out. She remembered suddenly that they hadn't yet even opened what remained of their presents.

"Hey, they have foot-long hot dogs," Melody said. "I'll have one of those, with lots of chili sauce."

"I guess I'll have one, too," Carole said slowly. It seemed a fitting conclusion to a miserable day. The new snow was all ugly slush now, and she was wet and dirty, and the day felt no more like Christmas than any other day. She wished she did not have to spend another minute with her cheerful, un-Christmasy family.

As if in answer to that wish, Gary's little car suddenly swung in beside them.

"Hi. I was on my way home and saw you parked here." He held up a little sack with drugstore markings. "Another tradition at our house. One

of us always has an upset stomach after dinner."
He gave Carole a sharp, questioning glance, as if
wondering how her attempts at tradition were
progressing.

"I—I'm really not very hungry," Carole said suddenly. "Would anyone mind if Gary dropped me
off at our house on his way home?"

She knew she had to get out of the car soon or
burst into tears right there in front of the family.
And she didn't want to hurt them; they couldn't
help being the way they were. She scooted out of
the car and slid into the seat beside Gary, who
still looked a little surprised.

"Well, merry Christmas, Mr. and Mrs. Brody,"
he called. "You, too, Melody." He was silent until
they swung into the stream of traffic on Central.
"I take it something happened to your plans."

"*Everything* happened to my plans." She told
him all that had gone wrong. "I guess I don't mind
so much that my Christmas tradition turned out to
be a big flop. It's just that no one but me even
cares that it was."

Gary braked at a red light. "Carole, did you ever
think," he said slowly, "that perhaps your family
has the nicest Christmas tradition of all?"

The nicest tradition, Carole scoffed silently.
*How can that be, when they haven't any traditions
at all? Hot dogs for dinner this year, no tree last*

year, no presents the year before.

"Mass confusion—that's the only tradition we have," she said lightly.

"Is it?"

Who else gave their Christmas dinner away? Carole asked herself. *Who else hadn't room for a tree because two other families shared the house? Who else hadn't any presents because they gave them all away? If that isn't mass confusion, what is it?*

The spirit of Christmas, that's what it was! Carole thought suddenly. Maybe her family did miss out on the traditions of tree and turkey and presents, but they had never yet missed out on the giving and sharing that were the real traditions of Christmas!

"Gary, would you— I mean, I think I'd like to go back to my family, after all. Would you take me there?" She smiled suddenly. "I didn't get to finish my hot dog."

Without another word, Gary swung the car around the block and back toward the drive-in. When he pulled in behind the Brody car, he suddenly leaned over and kissed her, before she had a chance to protest.

"An old Christmas tradition," he said softly. Then he added, with an impudent grin, "One I just started."

167

A BATCH OF THE BEST

Carole climbed into the car with her family, gave Gary a happy wave, and took a bite of her hot dog. They would probably have turkey before long, anyway, she decided philosophically. Perhaps her mother would fix one for Valentine's Day.

My Friend Carol

Myrna Blyth

IF BOTH our last names hadn't started with "G," I don't think Carol and I would have ever really known each other. We had nothing in common, you see. Nothing at all.

Carol and her friends were what I called the mindless ones—short, curvy girls with dimples, whose shoes were never run down at the heels. They failed exams, giggled helplessly when they didn't know an answer in class. But their hair would shine so in the school yard's sunshine, and their years of braces always ended in perfect, even, spaceless teeth. They were the girls who lived for just one thing—to be sixteen and have the big party and the permit that allowed them to drive.

My friends were different. We were the girls

who wrote the school paper, presided over the fine arts club, were determined to make honor society before the end of our sophomore year. We told each other we were "interesting looking . . . and that's a lot better than being pretty, isn't it?" That's what we told each other, but we couldn't tell that to ourselves. Our dreams were of college—Radcliffe? Swarthmore? Sarah Lawrence?—of trips to Europe, of the whole grown-up world where we would be beautiful, understood, and loved, at last.

Yes, there were two distinct groups in our sophomore class, two already-formed attitudes toward life that smiled vaguely at each other in the lunchroom and pointedly sat at separate tables. Natural, inevitable enemies, I felt, without even thinking about it—until the day Carol tried to become my friend.

She sat in front of me in homeroom. "Carol Gardner, Diane Geller . . ." the teacher had shouted briskly the first day of school. Too bad, I had thought idly, that my friends had end-of-the-alphabet names. Carol was in two of my classes, as well—geometry, where she could never prove anything, and English, where she avoided answering questions. She's dumb, I thought, whenever I thought about Carol. It doesn't matter if she's pretty and her hair always shines; she's dumb. A mindless one. Oh, let her have her dates and parties now. Now doesn't matter one single bit to me.

One morning in homeroom she turned to me and pointed to her lit book. "Diane," she whispered, "can you help me?"

I looked up from my Latin, trying to seem more annoyed than I actually was.

"Look here." She pointed to a page. "If Mark Antony is mad about Brutus killing Caesar, why does he keep saying he's an honorable man?"

Oh, how dense, I thought and nearly said it. "He's being ironic. Irony, you know." I turned back to the Gallic Wars.

Her face puckered, then she smiled. "I get it. Thanks." She smiled again. She really was a very pretty girl.

Of course, in class that day, Mr. Lucas asked Carol what device of rhetoric Mark Antony was using in his speech. Afterward she rushed over to me and grabbed my hand. "Oh, Di, did you hear? Did you hear? Thanks; you're swell!"

"What got into her?" one of my friends asked after Carol turned into the girls' room. I shrugged.

"I gave her the right answer," I laughed. "It's the only one she's ever had."

From then on, Carol began to talk to me in homeroom. She'd turn to ask a question or check a homework assignment. She even began to ask my advice about her dates.

171

"Should I go steady with Timmy? Do you think a college boy is too old for me?"

It was funny. Just because I knew more about geometry and literature, she thought I knew more about everything. What a joke. The theorem-proving Ann Landers, at your service. I wanted to shout at her, "I've had exactly five crummy dates in my entire life; nobody's asked me to go steady; so will you please leave me alone and stop making me feel bad?" But how could I say that? I was smart. It was my thing, my one thing. But I had to be smart all the time for Carol.

So I advised her—Diane, the sagacious—with considered sentences and a constant reliance on "What do *you* really want to do?"

For this I'd get her grateful smile the next day and her "I've thought about it, and you were right. Thanks, Di. Gee, you're swell!" Oh, Carol, Carol, so easy to advise.

She asked me to her house one day for lunch. "Please. Nella's made something good. I've told her I'd bring a friend."

"I'm not your friend," I wanted to say. But still I went. Her house was big, rambling, a white brick colonial on a tree-lined street. We went in through the kitchen. It smelled of cookies baking, cinnamon, brown sugar, the works. A big Negro woman in a white uniform stood over the stove, stirring. She smiled hello, showing shiny white teeth and a glittering gold cap. Really, it was just like that— a color advertisement for the good life.

"This is Diane, Nella. Where's Mom?"

"Hope you like clam chowder and hot cheese sandwiches, Diane. Your mom's upstairs. She's wanting you, Carol, honey."

I lived in a new, raw ranch house—picture window, small, square plot. My mother did the cooking and spent her afternoons in an endless pursuit of bargains. I had to hold the banister as I walked up those stairs.

Carol's mother sat at the dressing table, still in a housecoat but wearing lipstick. She was brushing her hair. She kissed Carol, took my hand, and never missed a stroke.

"Ninety-nine . . . one hundred. That's done. I have something to show you, darling." She opened a Florentine leather jewelry box and took out a velvet case. Inside lay a diamond necklace, heavy, cold, dazzling.

"Ohhh, Mommy," Carol murmured, letting out her breath. "It's gor-ge-ous, gor-ge-ous! Daddy's a jeweler," she explained, turning to me.

"The stock market's good," her mother laughed. She held the necklace to Carol's throat. "For me now. For you someday." They kissed each other.

173

I looked away. Can someone be wild with jealousy and sick with disgust at the same moment?

I hurried through my clam chowder and cheese sandwich and raced back to school, though Carol kept saying, "We've got time, Di, lots of time." Oh, no, no. Back I had to get to my lit and geometry, which diamond necklaces and spaceless teeth would never, never help Carol to understand.

That night I left my books and stared at myself in the mirror for a long time. Why wasn't my hair smooth and shiny and my nose short, too? Why didn't those stupid, ugly boys ever ask me out? It wasn't fair, that was all. There was no way to reason it out. I held a string of beads around my neck. "For me now. For you someday," I mimicked. Yes, for me someday, too. Just wait. I'd show her—them—everyone. My mother came into the room.

"Why don't you ever knock?" I said, throwing down the beads.

"What for?" She looked at me. "Oh, one of the moods, huh?"

"Just leave me alone. Leave me alone!" She went out, closing the door. I closed my eyes. For Carol it never had to change; and for me, would it ever, really?

Carol must have thought our lunch was a great success, because she began to wait for me after school. When I'd finish working on the paper, I'd find her at my locker.

"Cheerleading practice is over. Let's have a soda, Di. Treat you. Come on. Please." And again I went, to listen to Carol's troubles, to make jokes that I was sure I'd have to explain to her. Oh, I was superior as I sat chewing my straw and making pronouncements, for I still wasn't Carol's friend. She had so many things. She'd never have that.

With me, Carol, of course, was open, honest, confiding. I was smarter than her other friends. I could understand, explain so much more, she thought. She told me so many things about herself during those afternoons when we slowly sipped our drinks and watched the day grow dark. But mostly she talked about cheerleading.

Cheerleading was the most important thing in the world to Carol. About it she felt really deeply, almost passionately.

"I feel beautiful out there. Special and strong," she said to me once. "Everyone is looking at me and smiling—like with love. It's stupid, isn't it?"

I shrugged. "It really isn't stupid." But I didn't tell her why it wasn't. Even at this moment, when I felt close, almost tender toward Carol, I held back. I wouldn't share dreams.

She was the JayVee captain and terrified she

175

wouldn't make the varsity squad in spring tryouts. She begged me to come and watch her practice.

"You're the only friend I have who will be honest," she said. I, the great deceiver.

There was very little to say. She was a great cheerleader, even though I knew no one could be a great cheerleader. Cheerleaders were cute, bouncy, silly. But Carol had refined all this, without knowing it. She was the young girl wanting so much and achieving it with a leap.

After practice, she rushed toward me, her face anxious, her eyes trusting. "I'm no good, Di. Tell me the truth, tell me."

Here was the chance to say, "Carol, you're lovely, you're nice." My last chance. I heard my voice, reasonable, authoritative, firm. "I'm sure you'll make the squad, but. . . ." Oh, what was I thinking of—a diamond necklace, a mother who kissed you softly, dates every Saturday night? And still she was grateful.

All in the same week in March, Carol would turn sixteen, give a party, have cheerleading tryouts, and get her driving permit.

"They're going to give me a convertible for my birthday. Ohhh . . . I'll never live through the excitement. . . . What if I don't make cheering! Mom says we can go to Bergdorf's to shop for my dress for the party."

176

Carol's party was held at the country club to which her family belonged. Of course, I was invited. No one else I knew well went. The party was sumptuous, unbelievable. The dining room of the club was a mass of pink and white roses, everywhere you looked. A band played; a comedian told jokes. Waiters swooped, bringing platters of thick roast beef and, finally, an enormous pink and white whipped cream cake. "Happy birthday, darling Carol." Everyone sang, laughed, danced, kissed Carol. She stood on the bandstand, her dark hair high and shining, wearing a white lace dress, sashed in pink. A diamond glittered at her throat. She looked beautiful.

It's a rite for a vestal virgin, I thought, unable to confide my observation to anyone else at the party, before a sacrifice.

"It's the best sweet sixteen I've ever been to," decided Bonny, one of Carol's mindless friends. "I'll be honest—it's better than my own."

I watched Carol all night as she danced gaily with her father, laughed and flirted with the boys she dated. She felt special, I knew, and everyone was smiling at her with love. When she came to my table, she hugged me tightly and kissed me on the cheek. "I'm so happy," she whispered. "Oh, Di, Di, I never felt so happy."

I wanted to say something polite and distant,

but I couldn't. Her face was too eager. "It's a lovely party," I said. "A wonderful party." Carol hugged me again.

"Come on, dance!" she said to the boy sitting next to me. He took my hand. Carol had made him ask me, in some subtle way I couldn't even follow. I should have been angry and offended, but Carol was smiling so brightly. She was trying to be nice, especially nice to me. Oh, what was the use of protesting? I let the boy lead me to the dance floor.

Later, when I was dancing again, Carol passed me. "Are you having a good time?" she mouthed.

"Oh, yes, yes, yes," I exulted. I couldn't stand apart. It was just like a color advertisement, and I was in the corner of the picture for a few hours.

In the morning, when I called Carol to say thanks, Nella answered and said Carol was in bed and couldn't get up.

"She woke up a little sick and feverish today, Diane. All the excitement, I suppose. Poor child. The doctor's coming."

"Tell her the party was fun." Well, it was, in its way. "And give her my best."

Carol didn't come to school on Monday or Tuesday. She'll be here tomorrow, I assured myself, looking at her empty desk. Wednesday was the first day of cheerleading tryouts. That night I felt I should call. Her mother answered the phone.

"Oh, Diane. We're just on the way out. We're taking Carol to the hospital. She's a very sick little girl."

"But what's wrong?" I felt a little frightened.

"Some respiratory infection. I must go. Goodbye, dear."

"Tell her. . . ." But what was the use? The line was broken, and by that time Carol wouldn't have been able to understand what I suddenly wanted to tell her.

All Wednesday we talked about her at school. "There's nothing to worry about," I assured her friends. They clustered about me, their perfectly made-up faces creased with concern. "Not with all the drugs we have today. Penicillin, all the mycins. . . ." I reeled off the long, comforting names.

"If she doesn't come to school tomorrow, she won't make cheerleading," her friends babbled.

"It's stupid to even think about that now—now that she's so sick," I told them irritably. But I had thought the same thing.

Oh, they'll let her try out in a couple of weeks, I told myself. All Carol wanted was to be a cheerleader. It was such a little dream. Such a little thing to want. It would be easy for her to have.

On Thursday we all knew Carol was in an oxygen tent and was having trouble breathing. The teachers whispered about it in the halls. We made phone calls to the hospital between classes. There was no change in her condition all day.

At three I went to the newspaper office. I started to edit an article, but I couldn't concentrate. I was just gathering my books together when Bonny came in. Her face was red, wet, and shiny. She looked at me, her eyes red and blurred with tears.

"Carol's dead!"

My mind went white. I stood up and stared at her matted, smeared eyelashes. I pointed my arm at her.

"You're a stupid, stupid girl," I shrieked. "How dare you make such a joke!"

She recoiled and started sobbing. "But it's true, it's true. She's dead. She is."

Mr. Lucas came into the room and looked from one of us to the other—from me, standing, my arm out, rigid, seeing nothing, to Bonny, gurgling and cowering in the corner.

He eased my arm down. "She died about two thirty, Diane. It's terrible, terrible," he murmured. I rushed past him then, to the girls' room, where I was sick.

I couldn't cry that night or the next morning before the funeral. I lay in my bed and heard my

181

mother make phone call after phone call.

"Isn't it something?" She tried to whisper, but I could always hear her. "She's being buried exactly one week after her sweet sixteen. Isn't that just awful?" I'd be sick over and over, but I couldn't cry.

Bonny drove me to the funeral, chattering and weeping. "They say she knew. . . . She begged her mother to help her. . . . She talked about cheerleading, too." Bonny paused to wipe her eyes. "Once when she slept at my house, we talked about dying. She was so quiet. . . ."

Yes, she'd be quiet. I could see Carol's face when she read a problem she couldn't understand —her face puckered, her expression almost hurt. Is this how she finally fell asleep?

The funeral parlor was crowded with girls, boys, teachers. I wouldn't go up to the coffin. Bonny whispered to me, "She's wearing the lace and pink dress. A diamond necklace. She looks beautiful." I wanted to grab Bonny, pinch her, and tell her to stop being disgusting. But could I judge her grief? Could I tell her how to show it? I covered my face with my hands and turned away.

The next night, Bonny and I and a few teachers went to see Carol's parents. I just felt I had to go. They were in their darkened living room. Her mother sat on the couch. She wore no makeup, and her face was old. She'd begin to talk about Carol, but tears would well up in her eyes, and her voice would fade away. Carol's father sat silent beside her. He wore his jeweler's glasses high on his forehead and kept looking at the floor.

Nella, red-eyed, dressed in black, carried around plates of cakes, cups of tea and coffee. The teachers ate quickly, placing each crumb they dropped neatly on their napkins. I drank my coffee, tried to chew a dry cookie. I had to get out of there. Abruptly I crossed the room, knocking against a table as I walked, hearing the shudder of dishes. At the door, Carol's mother took my hand. "Carol liked you so much. Respected you. It meant so much to her to have you as a friend." I couldn't say a word.

That night, when I finally fell asleep, I dreamed of Carol. She wore her lace dress, and diamonds glittered from her hair and neck and hands. She stood in a crowd of people and smiled at me. I chased after her, calling. I had so much to say to her. "Carol, Carol," I screamed in my dream, "listen to me." But the crowd was still far away as I ran. And when I got there—where?—it was empty, silent, and I was awake, lying in my cold bed.

Then, finally, I cried. I cried for Carol and for the things that she expected and would never have —a cheerleader's costume, a driver's license, a

183

wedding gown. Oh, Carol, you only wanted what every girl should have! This is what I loathed you for. Such little dreams were sure to come true. How stupid and cruel I was. I was the shallow, narrow one. I hated you as the image of all I didn't have . . . and I couldn't see you as a girl—only as an image. But now a girl is dead. Now it is ended for you. Nothing matters—not my friendship or a yellow sweater or a boy to kiss. There is nothing.

I went to the window. Snow, the last of the winter, was falling softly, softly, over all. The tears on my cheeks grew as cold as diamonds. For you now, for me someday; only this future is sure. Good or bad, whatever it is, life is in the moment. I watched the snow and cried through the night for my friend.

The Real Me

Pat Carlson

I guess it was natural that I should think of Lester at that miserable moment, because the same thing was happening all over again. There I was, rattled and wavering, at the top of the very same steps, wanting to run, praying for the courage to stay and say something so right to a boy that it would change my whole life.

How long ago was it? Four years. I was in the eighth grade at Andrew Jackson Junior High at the time. He hadn't been important since, but I remembered him, the way you remember all the people who were the first: the first good friend, the first enemy—the first boy you fall in love with.

Lester came around a lot that year, flexing his

muscles, hanging off the porch rail, and chinning himself on Mother's stone geranium pot that swung on chains over the steps. His act was really for Kate Mary.

Kate Mary's mother and mine were sisters. Both our families had always lived in a big two-family flat on Elroy Street, Kate Mary upstairs and I downstairs. For a while, our mothers dressed us alike, and forever more, I supposed, they'd compare us: shoe sizes, knee scars, head bumps—rings on fingers. . . .

Since he couldn't perform outside Kate Mary's window, Lester used the porch for a stage, and since Kate Mary seldom paid him any attention, he used me for an audience.

I was impressed with everything about Lester, from his high-school status to the graceful way he lit matches with his murky thumbnail. I'd see his scarlet jersey, with "Wildcats" printed across the chest, coming down Elroy Street, and I'd trip over myself getting to the top porch step, where I'd sit and try to look as if I just happened to be there at the moment he happened along.

We spent a lot of time on that porch, Lester and I, while he waited for Kate Mary to wander in or out and perhaps notice he was alive—and while I waited for him to notice I was among the living. One day we were both successful.

186

Kate Mary came out the door with two bags of pop bottles. When she took back empties, it meant she was bankrupt and desperate. She looked around for Bingo Callahan or some of her other satellites, to give her a hand. They were usually there. Our porch gathered boys the way a vacuum snaps up tacks. Kate Mary seldom had to carry her own pop bottles. This time, she saw nobody but Lester, dangling hopefully off the geranium pot, but I guess he didn't register with her, even though he spoke up and said, "Hi, Kate Mary!" in a loud, cracked voice.

"Hi," she said vaguely and staggered down the street with her bottles. Lester dropped onto the steps below me, dejected and wounded. I rummaged for something to say, something consoling and more memorable than "My, but you're strong!" Now was certainly the time for it.

He cracked his knuckles, while the heat in my brain climbed higher. Any second he'd go, maybe never to return. If I could think of something flattering, something to make him notice me. . . . I leaned down and blurted recklessly, "Can you crack a Brazil nut in your bare hand?"

"Huh?" said Lester.

"Well . . . I just thought . . . you might. I heard of somebody who could, and you'd have to be pretty strong to do that, so . . . it made me think

187

of you." I floundered, but I got it out.

Lester's face slowly took on a pleased expression. Oh, joy, I'd said the right thing! "Yeah, I guess I could," he admitted. "Y'know, some guys can't get a good grip on a football. Their hands are too small, but I can really wrap around one."

"I can believe it," I burbled, admiring the oversize paws he stretched out for my inspection. Timidly I reached out and measured my hand against his. Palms touching, we both flushed, but Lester pulled his manhood together and did his part. His fingers swallowed my hand. I gave him a surprised smile. He moved closer, and then I realized what I was doing. I was *flirting*. This was what Kate Mary did while yawning, riding a bicycle, breathing, and sleeping soundly. I'd finally learned how —and with a boy who liked her kind of girl!

Lester leaned nearer, his hand growing moist and warm, his full attention riveted on me. I'd made him forget everything else in the world. My brain swam with the heady power of it.

I knew success of the purest kind—for one fleeting moment—then it turned to ashes. Down the street, Kate Mary turned back. Lester's presence must have suddenly registered with her, like a mathematical formula: Boy plus muscle equals bottle carrier. She came toward us, with the beginning of her smile blazing. It lit her up from the

top of her blue black head to the dimple in her chin, and, in between, those violet eyes danced at Lester. My heart sank so fast that I felt it bounce when it hit bottom. Lester jerked to his feet, arms and legs out of control with eagerness.

"I don't think I can get these to the store alone. You wouldn't be going my way, would you, Lester?" Kate Mary cooed at him.

"Sure!" he cried, forgetting I'd ever been born, and scrambled to her side.

Right then, I wished I could bite my thumb at her and declare a vendetta, like the Pasquales and their cousins, the Albertinos, up the block. A big, satisfactory hate would help no end, but Kate Mary was hard to hate on a permanent basis. She almost never bothered to think, but the emotions that took the place of her brain were lightning-fast and soft as butter. She saw my face, and, in a flash, she grasped what was going on inside me and, worse, what she'd done.

Her arms relaxed around the bagged bottles, deliberately letting them smash on the sidewalk. "Look at that," she said dully, while her eyes asked my pardon. "I just knew I wouldn't make it."

I watched Lester picking up the glass, scurrying around her feet like a puppy. When I couldn't stand it another second, I lifted my chin off my fists and went inside, trying very hard to sweep the rejected feeling out of myself.

It was an experience, I told myself gloomily, and if there was one thing I was missing, it was experience. I'd learned a couple of things, hadn't I? Not to waste my heart on Lester, and how to flirt—a little.

I shut the door of my room and stood still, imagining a boy's face coming closer, closer—but not Lester's. He'd cut me to the quick, or at least deep enough to give *him* up for eternity. Maybe somebody a little like him, though; a lordly, athletic tiger. All right, I was doomed to plain brown hair and calico eyes, but behind them—if a person looked—there might be something interesting, even different, just waiting. Someday a better man than Lester would notice it. When he did, I hoped Kate Mary would be far, far away.

She was right beside me, as usual, when we finished junior high that June. The writer of the Class Will gave extra space to the legacies Kate Mary left the next graduating class. Her smile, he wrote, went to Dimples Novak, her hair to Sophia Albertino, her eyes to Nancy Mulvaney. He left my brain to the Math Club.

I plodded drearily into high school. It's a time of great depression for some people, especially people who go into it prelabeled "Good Student," "No Behavior Problem," and "Shy"!

My mother gave me worried advice: "Be outgoing, dear. Join the cheerleaders. Oh, the fun *I* had! Well, join *some*thing!"

Aunt Anne made little suggestions: "Sew glitter on your sweaters; smile more, Annie. Be *interested* in people!"

Uncle Tim rumbled, "Look alive, Annie! Speak up and let the world know you're here!"

"It's glands," my father announced hopefully. "Some people have slow glands. She won't *stay* this way."

When they weren't talking at me, they were talking about me, and how they could talk! They'd never had tongue trouble, not one of them. They had only to open their mouths, and new friends fell in. The family tree was tirelessly examined around the kitchen table. No, there wasn't a bashful soul in it. Where could it have come from, this quiet oddity that was Annie?

I wasn't quiet with Franklin. I could have told them that, but any mention of him brought a "Yekh!" from Kate Mary and a disappointed sigh from my mother. They'd rejected him at first glance.

I found Franklin under the bleachers on Field Day. He was supposed to be out on the field, displaying his physical fitness. I could see right away he didn't have any, and that was why he was there, hiding his hundred and three pounds under leaves and candy wrappers.

I'd been waiting to exhibit my grace on the trampoline, where I'd bounce all alone, the only thing in action, entertaining four thousand eyes. I peered at the eyes and panicked. The next thing, I was under the bleachers, meeting Franklin.

It was a quick friendship, what with being fugitives together and a few other things we found out about each other. We could talk. That was the main thing. We talked about extrasensory perception and desert islands and how we'd both like to join the Israeli army for one of their wars.

Franklin's father worried about his glands, too. He was built like a short straw—just nothing, at least, not yet. The only place he was a giant was in class.

In our junior year, we talked about economics. Franklin swam through that class as if he'd hit his natural element, and I was fascinated with it, too. I don't remember which of us really invented BOOM, but it enthralled us from the minute we thought of it.

BOOM had more moves than chess and more rules than baseball. It started out as a simple exercise in stock market investment, then switched

193

into a corporation game, with proxy fights, mergers, and antitrust suits. By the time it expanded into international trade, its homemade boards and counters covered our rec room floor. BOOM required at least twelve players with total recall.

"It's like one of those jelly-blob monsters from Planet Y, devouring the earth," I marveled.

"Yes, but we'd make a million on this—if we could just get it under control," Franklin said.

I was happy with Franklin—and ashamed of it.

"Throw him back, Annie. He's undersized!" Uncle Tim advised.

"Listen, dear, if you spend every date night playing games with that kind of boy, it'll ruin your reputation!" Aunt Anne warned, as if Franklin were smothered in vices. "The boys who count will think you're—well—square, like him. You're known by the company you keep!"

"You can do better than that little owl!" Kate Mary insisted. Overwhelmed, I tried my desperate best that summer, when Kate launched herself into a bigger project than BOOM: bringing out what she said was the real me just yearning to hatch.

Franklin went off to Arizona with a kid from school whose archaeologist father was taking them along on his job. BOOM was stuffed into the dusty storeroom with our old twin stroller and identical high chairs—and I hatched a nervous imitation of Kate Mary.

I didn't feel right, chattering and bubbling off the top of my head, but it gave me a protective mask to wear with the dates her dates fixed up for me. They were second-string boys, the hero-worshiping, hanger-on buddies of the wheels she went with. When they spoke at all, they told me what a great guy old Steve or old Ken or old Bingo was, but mostly they were mute.

Sometimes, for relief, I thought about the less painful complications of BOOM and added pieces to it. They grew to quite a pile in the storeroom. I needed a lot of relief.

When school reopened, Kate Mary tried a new method: unplanned impulse—or maybe it was delirium. She came down with twenty-four hour flu the day of the school's traditional September Welcome Dance. Her temperature was 103° when she tottered downstairs to tell me I was going in her place. "With Bingo Callahan?" I cried.

"Sure; I called him. It's the best idea I ever had!" she beamed. "Don't you *see?* Whatever Bingo does, the other boys do. Look what happened when he got a crew cut for sports. Presto! Short hair all over the place! Is that power, or is that raw power? One date with Bingo and you're

195

in. Talk about brilliant!"

"Talk about what Bingo said," I suggested.

"Hurry and get ready! You haven't much time," Kate Mary hedged and flapped hastily back to her bed.

The house went up in a flurry the minute her mother and mine realized what was happening. The family got it into their heads that this was my night to hatch, that while I was off with Bingo, some mysterious process would change me to enchanting, kicky, and captivating. Even my father kept saying he'd *told* everybody I'd blossom one of these days, and this was it.

Seniors went formal, and I'd never had occasion to buy a formal of my own. They bustled me into Kate Mary's lime green. It didn't fit. Probably my glands again, I thought. They were definitely more backward than Kate's. A few tucks and some judicious padding made the dress presentable.

"Glad you could come, Anne. I'd have had to go stag," Bingo said, looking as if he'd rather have. After that, his conversation fell down and died before we got out of the driveway. I tried shocking it back to life with my imitation Kate Mary chatter-and-bubble. Bingo's eyes rolled uneasily.

I saved my breath and plunged into the dances with furious energy, hoping somebody would please notice my verve and take me off his hands.

In the midst of my verve, I saw Franklin! It was the first time I'd seen him since late spring. He was late getting back from his summer job—and he wasn't the same Franklin.

He was taller, more cowboy-lean than straw-thin, and tanned to mahogany. His smile flashed confidently at the girl in his arms—Jo Sloan, debating team, Latin club, student council—also smooth and relaxed. He'd not only learned to dance; he'd also learned to get a girl like that!

If Aunt Anne could see him now, she wouldn't be so quick to call him square. I'm only pretending I've changed, but he has, I thought miserably. He's outgrown me!

He saw me standing there, waiting for Bingo to come back from giving somebody a friendly punch in the arm. He pulled Jo swiftly across the floor to me. She had an easy poise and callouses on her hands. "They're from digging," she said, laughing. "Frank and I were laborers in an old Indian pit house. We sat on our heels all summer and scraped up broken pottery for a museum."

So this was the kid from school with the archaeologist father. "What fun," I said coldly and hated myself.

"It was fun, especially the teaching part," Franklin told me. "The Indian kids used to come and watch us and drink our Coca-Cola. When it

197

was too hot to work, Jo and I taught school. Told 'em about the rest of the world and why people in other places live differently. Sometimes I got the feeling we were getting through, making them see it. Oh, it was a great summer!"

"Mine was great, too," I said and went on about my whirling social life, wishing Bingo would hurry back to prove it. I just had no time anymore, I declared, chattering recklessly but unable to stop. Maybe I'd have gone on forever, a record babbling on the wrong rpm, if Franklin's left eyebrow hadn't lifted, surprised and definitely cool.

It closed my throat and stopped the flood. I'd never seen him do that before. It looked so adult. He was my old friend—and yet he wasn't. I felt like an intruder on Jo's claim—or worse, the kiddie playmate he'd had in the long ago.

"I've heard so much about you and BOOM. I'd love to see it. Have you made any headway with it this summer?" Jo spoke into the sudden silence.

"Oh, *that*—that little game." I flicked her question aside, fluttering vivaciously over her shoulder at nobody. "It must be in the storeroom somewhere. I never get time to look at it."

"Oh? Well, since you're so busy now, maybe I'd better take it home. Tomorrow's Saturday. I could pick it up in the morning," Franklin said.

I was being divorced—and he was running off

with the baby! "Sure," I said, while my who-cares smile hurt clear to my ears, "anytime. There's Bingo! See you later. He's looking for me."

Bingo *was* dutifully glancing around for me, and, just as dutifully, he danced with me. Oh, what a bitter night this was turning out to be.

"Let 'em know you're there!" Dad had urged.

"Have *fun* now," Mother had said, smiling.

"Let yourself go!" Kate Mary had ordered.

I gave it a ferocious try, but it was the dress that let go, to the beat of three guitars and a hot drum. The hasty tucks popped, the hem dropped, and the improvised bustline padding bulged around my lower ribs. The real, kicky, captivating me shrank, shriveled, and vanished.

My brain was the real surprise. It held up. "This is what they call a traumatic experience," it lectured calmly. "Escape *now*, or be marked for life!"

Bingo already was marked. I stepped from his flaccid grip, completely through my hem, and fell out the nearest door.

I kept going, scurrying from shadow to shadow, a wounded creature of the night, streaking for its burrow. I could never again face Bingo, Franklin, *any*body I knew, or even the light of day!

I huddled on our steps, soaking the tatters of Kate Mary's formal with my tears. Pictures of myself at the dance kept flashing across the inside of my forehead. It wasn't just the dress. I had been awful—and everybody had seen the awfulness—the way I'd acted with Franklin, the way I'd acted, period! The bounce that didn't match the panicky eyes, the frantic smiling, the gabble—they had no business coming out of me. None of them *belonged* in me!

"Out of character" was the right descriptive phrase. It was a favorite with my last year's English teacher. Strange, jolting things happened when a character stepped out of character. She stopped growing and just stood around jangling and getting on everybody's nerves. Maybe I had no character to step out of, but I'd sure tried to step *into* the wrong one. I'd been Cinderella, parading in a ball gown—and here I was, back in rags, where I belonged!

"I don't fit!" I sobbed to the geranium pot. "I don't fit with any of them. Not with my own family, and not even with Franklin anymore!"

"Anne—uh, Annie, are you all right?" a shadow mumbled from a car parked at the curb. Bingo! He'd sped here ahead of me, had seen my whole performance!

I'd scream, "Go away!" and run. I'd rather die than see him. I'd rather die than—go on being somebody I didn't have two pins of respect for.

That's when I thought of Lester. Here I'd sat,

nerving myself to say something to make him no-
tice me. If I managed it, it would change the world
for me. I'd managed it—for a couple of minutes—
and wasted all the years since, trying to be a tiger's
mate.

I hadn't enjoyed a second of it, hadn't meshed
with a single one of the "tigers." If there was a
real me buried under the debris of my shattered
life, she'd better surface quickly, and she'd better
be somebody I could face in the morning!

Up she came, as shaky as a colt on new legs, but
I wasn't ashamed of her when she spoke up.
"Bingo, I—I'm sorry I made a big jerk of myself
and embarrassed you in front of everybody." I
wiped my face on the formal's scratchy skirt. It
wasn't very absorbent. He sat beside me and put
his handkerchief in my hand. "You won't be running into me much anymore," I assured him. "I'm
going to give up school and get a job Monday, so
I'm fine, and you can go home now."

He didn't go home. He cleared his throat and
said, "I quit school once. Sixth grade. We lived
on the north side then. My dad was sick that year,
and with a family of five girls and a boy—man,
were we broke! Mom got to be a genius at making
things over. She even ripped up my older sister's
gym suit and sewed it into gym shorts for me. They
looked okay, navy blue and all, but when I put

them on in the locker room, there was this elastic still in the legs. All the guys saw it. It took my folks three days to talk me out of our cellar and back to school. I was going to be a hermit down there. I never told this before, but nobody called me Bingo till I was sinking baskets in junior high. Before that, I was—Bloomers Callahan. I can laugh about it now. Watch."

He gave a forced ha-ha and suggested, "Now you try."

It was the least I could do. I choked out a couple of ha-has. Some unexpected nervous ones followed, and then we were both laughing, deep and hard. It was insane at a time like this.

"It won't take you three days to come out of the cellar, will it, Annie?" he asked when we'd sobered down.

I thought about that, wanting to be honest. I was through pretending to courage or anything else I didn't have, but his pep talk deserved better than failure. He'd never confessed to a soul about his bloomers till I needed to hear it. He hadn't even stayed behind at the dance long enough to tell his friends, "She wasn't *my* idea of a date. I dragged her as a favor to Kate Mary," erasing his embarrassment with their sympathy. He probably wouldn't think of it. Bingo didn't need to be patted on the back and told he was still a tiger. He just was one, through and through, the nicest, kindest, biggest tiger of them all.

"I guess I'll have to, won't I? Go back, I mean, and live it down," I answered slowly.

Kate Mary was lucky to have him, and it was startling to realize that I was decently glad she did have him. Beautiful as he was, no one like him could be my cup of tea. We weren't natural companions. I was a misfit in Kate Mary's world. Too bad I hadn't admitted it years before. Too bad my family—darn them, anyway—hadn't admitted it ahead of me. Oh, the pain it would have saved!

"Do you know what it's like to be the only different one in a family and all of them steering you wrong?" I burst out.

"I've got five sisters," Bingo reminded me, "so I was born different. My dad thought sports were kid stuff, and my mother had her heart set on me being a lawyer. I'm going to be a coach."

"That must be rough," I sympathized.

He shook his head. "Not so bad. I believe in what I'm doing. It suits me, so now it suits them, too. First they got used to it, and then they got proud of me."

And there it was, very simple and very direct. I had to respect my own ways and my own ideas, before anyone else would. I had to be me.

I got up and faced our front door. That was the

first step. "Good night, Bingo—and thanks."

"For a nice time?" He grinned.

"For saving my life—I think," I told him.

They were gathered around our kitchen table, expectant, sparkly-eyed—even Kate Mary, wrapped in a blanket. I entered, red-nosed and raggedy-hemmed. It was sad. My mother cried for me. I cried because she cried. My father blamed glands, and Aunt Anne blamed the dress to cheer me up. "If you'd just had the right size, or if we'd had time to alter it better. . . ." Everybody chimed in loyally. Oh, yes, if only, if only . . . it all would have been different.

I wanted to tell them no dress would make me into Kate Mary, but they wouldn't have given up hope. Not yet. They'd have to see for themselves. It was enough, for now, that I knew.

The next morning, I went down to the storeroom and tenderly sorted BOOM, clearing it of the summer's dust. I wanted it to look its best. Then I sat cross-legged beside the untidy mammoth and mourned. It was like parting with something alive. Not that I loved it exactly, but I'd been so happy in those hours of invention and so happy with—

"Franklin! I'd hardly know you," my mother cried upstairs.

"My, how you've grown this summer!" That was Aunt Anne's voice, almost approving.

"*Now* they decide he's passable!" I muttered bitterly. "I wish he were still an owl! Then maybe this wouldn't be happening."

I wrapped my arms tight around my knees and watched him come down the stairs. I *wouldn't* feel embarrassed about last night. We were strangers, so what did it matter? In ten minutes, we'd be saying good-bye forever.

He circled twice around BOOM, sneaking glances at me as if I were an unfamiliar species that might bite. *Oh, take it and go,* I wished silently. *Just don't say anything.*

"It *is* a monster. It grew!" he said.

"I added a little," I mumbled.

"Thought you were too busy," he reminded me.

I opened my mouth to say I'd had an occasional split second, when I wasn't being the belle of the beach, but my ego was gone. At least, the old ego was, dead and buried in its borrowed skin.

"I lied," I said and felt a soaring liberty. Why, there was freedom in being myself. Pure, sweet freedom!

"Annie?" Franklin said, and he squatted on his heels to peer into my face, looking like a desert Indian. "You really *haven't* gone all funny on me, have you? Jo told me it was an act, but I wasn't sure."

I froze at the mention of her name. How dare

she see straight through me!

"Jo got the idea of throwing a BOOM party tonight," he announced.

" 'The ides of March are come,' " I muttered under my breath. "Oh, treachery! Oh, the end!"

"If we invite kids who take to this kind of thing, they might solve some of the bugs," he said. "It'll be different, anyway. We've got quite a few lined up so far."

I unraveled my sweat shirt sleeve, giving it my deepest attention. If he invited me to watch him date Jo, I was liable to go *very* all funny on him.

"I told Jo you'd be too busy, but she said—uh— she thought you might—if I asked you to come with me," he said.

"With you?"

"If you're not too busy," he added. "You'd know most of the kids from school, except for the guy Jo likes."

"The guy Jo likes?" I echoed, much too high.

"He's starting college in a couple of days, and he's kind of stuffy about it. He wouldn't take her to our dinky high school dance last night, but she says BOOM will impress him. I think he's majoring in how to be a tycoon," Franklin explained.

"It was nice of you to take her," I said, yanking my voice down, along with half my shirt cuff.

"No, I wanted to go out and see people again,

but we'd just got home from Arizona, so I couldn't expect to get a date with—uh—anybody else."

I wondered if I could start over and give Jo a better image of me—something on the natural side. I could like that girl! "Sure, I'll come. I think it's a great idea. Why didn't we think of it before?" I laughed, patting BOOM.

"We weren't ready before," Franklin said, very seriously.

There was a snag. BOOM wouldn't fit in Franklin's little car, especially not the main piece, which was an old grand piano lid. "Could we have the party here?" I asked.

We had the party in our rec room, where BOOM was born. It was nothing like Kate Mary's parties. Certainly nothing like it had ever happened to my family.

"Simplify!" yelled the editor of the school paper. "Listen, it can be a commercial success if they cut out the petty details and divide it into five separate games!"

"Cut out?" screamed the guy Jo liked, above nine other bloodless arguments. "They *forgot* half of what makes the world go round! Where's inflation, slump, strikes, and where—*where* are corporate taxes?"

I unleashed passionate opinions on the Federal

Reserve System, unions, whither Christianity, the Supreme Court, and why Desdemona couldn't stitch herself up another strawberry hankie to show Othello. And they listened—with interest. It was like landing on shore at last, after years at sea, and finding the natives friendly. These were my people. I belonged.

I knew it for sure when I went upstairs for more food and saw the family's faces. They were drinking coffee at the kitchen table, awed at the hubbub below. "Guess we won't have to tell you anymore to speak up, Annie. We heard you down there." Uncle Tim grinned.

"Glands, that's what does it when the right time comes. I told you!" Dad nodded.

"They're nice kids. Different—but nice," Aunt Anne conceded.

"Annie's friends aren't kids, exactly. They're more like people," Mother boasted, as if she'd invented them.

The only stamp of approval missing was Kate Mary's. I'd forgotten her! I raced upstairs and stopped dead halfway. She could have come without my asking her. Maybe she was afraid of spoiling it for me. She would, too. She couldn't help it. That's just the way things were. Who'd I think I was kidding with this little moment of false glory? When the boys in the rec room got one look at her,

I'd go wallflower again. It would be her party, swinging her way.

I almost turned around, but she'd never had a party without urging me to come, though I was no asset to them. I couldn't sneak off and leave her. I went the rest of the way on lead legs.

She was listening to records and staring at the ceiling. "Don't you feel well enough to come down? It must be lonesome up here," I said, fighting to be brave about it.

She blinked at me with a sour grin. Finally she said, "It's more lonesome at your party. I've *been* down. Nobody noticed me—not after I opened my mouth, anyway. Do you know what Ben Williams said to Karen Mills when he thought I was gone? 'She's a doll, but she sure can't carry on much of a conversation!'"

"Oh, Kate, that's crazy!" I gasped.

"That's what I thought," she murmured. "It hurt my feelings for a minute, but then I remembered that one of *my* friends said almost the same thing about you. Annie, we're just not each other's type!"

"And it only took seventeen years to notice it," I sighed.

She giggled. "Go on back to your party. And when we have kids, let's never buy them a twin stroller!"

"Never!" I promised and hoped my children

wouldn't mind waiting awhile. There were a lot of things I wanted to do first. Franklin talked about that after the others left, while we were clearing away the mess.

"If we cut it up into simple games, it might pay our whole way through college," he said as we stacked BOOM.

"I've thought of it before, but I was afraid you'd feel it was a kind of sacrilege," I told him.

He shook his head. "We're going in the same direction, Annie, into real economics, and that's no game. It's people—their homes, their schools, their sicknesses, and their bread and butter. I learned that from the Indian kids. Besides"—he grinned at me—"I think *you're* more interesting than corporate taxes, so we couldn't go on just playing BOOM much longer, could we?"

The back of my neck tingled. I was shy about facing him. He wasn't what I'd dreamed of—the lordly tiger crushing Brazil nuts in his bare hands —and the instant I looked at him, he'd know how glad I was that dreams seldom come true. So glad that I could fly!

The real me, close to full-grown now, gave an impatient shove. "Go on," she urged. "This *is* my night to hatch!" I turned to meet his eyes.

Acknowledgments

"LITTLE SISTER WILL LEAD YOU" by Pauline Smith. Reprinted from *Twelve/Fifteen,* November 20, 1966. Copyright © 1966 by Graded Press.

"SUNDAY AFTERNOON" by Lucile Vaughan Payne. Copyright © 1949 by Lucile Vaughan Payne. Appeared originally in *Seventeen®*. Reprinted by permission of McIntosh and Otis, Inc.

"NOT EXACTLY CARNABY STREET" by Jane Williams Pugel. Copyright 1969 by *American Girl.* Appeared originally in *American Girl,* April, 1969. Reprinted by permission of the *American Girl,* a magazine for all girls, published by Girl Scouts of the U.S.A.

"THE FRIENDS" by Sofi O'Bryan. Copyright 1966 by Super Market Publishing Co., Inc., a subsidiary of MacFadden-Bartell Corporation, New York, N. Y. Appeared originally in *In* magazine, June, 1966.

"THE SENSATIONAL TYPE" by Shirley Shapiro Pugh. Copyright © 1950 by Triangle Publications, Inc. for *Seventeen®*. Reprinted from *Seventeen®* with permission of the author.

"THE BLUE PROMISE" by Loretta Strehlow. Copyright 1966 by the *American Girl,* a magazine for all girls, published by Girl Scouts of the U.S.A. Reprinted from *American Girl,* July, 1966, by permission of the author and Larry Sternig Literary Agency.

"MR. DILLON RIDES AGAIN" by Lorena K. Sample. Reprinted from *Twelve/Fifteen,* January 28, 1968. Copyright © 1967 by Graded Press.